HEATHER BOYD

BESTSELLING AUTHOR

MISS MAYHEM ✦ BOOK 3

MISS RADLEY'S THIRD DARE

Chapter One

There is nothing like having a *past* to shake up a happy present.

Julia Radley flopped onto her bed and groaned into her pillow. The concept of being so grievously ruined because of her harmless little dare three months ago had not truly occurred to her at the time Valentine Merton had accepted the challenge. She had thought any scandal would have blown over soon after the event that proved her an equal to a man when it came to swimming fast. To her dismay, all these months later, she had become a target of her brother's unending fury and society's scorn.

She had to escape.

"Don't you dare walk away from me, young lady," Linus, her brother and constant pain in her side, bellowed as he followed into her bedchamber to continue delivering his latest assessments of her predicament from the doorway. "You have no idea what strain this places upon me. What this has done to me. And—"

"What have I done to you?" She sat up, blowing a lock of red hair from her eyes. "All I have done is determined that I can swim faster than one man. Just one member of the male gender to prove my point that women possess more skills than merely wielding a needle. I did not parade myself around in my undergarments for the benefit of the masses. The entire event took no more than half an hour and you act like it is such a long-lasting disaster. You were there. You saw everything and said nothing at the time."

"How could I have stopped you when I was the last to know my sister had been conspiring with a neighbor behind my back?" Linus turned an unhealthy shade of puce when he referred to her opponent, Valentine Merton. Once he'd called the man his best friend, but no more. Not since the race had they been seen together. "Everyone tried to prevent the race. If you were a lady in any shape or form, no one in Brighton would have any idea of what you look like underneath that gown. As it is—"

A loud knock pounded on the door one floor below them and Linus glanced over his shoulder swiftly.

At last, a caller had come to distract Linus from his daily lecture before he really got going. She held her breath as her brother turned on his heel and marched downstairs without another word.

Julia flopped onto her back as Mr. Walter George's measured tones reached her with an invitation to go out. She grinned and sent Mr. George her undying gratitude. Her brother's other friends were very good at distracting Linus when he was in high alt. So good, she might even be able to sneak out of the house to visit with Mr. George's sister Imogen for a good long while without her brother knowing.

The front door slammed shut and Julia jumped to her feet, snatched up her best shawl and checked her reflection in the mirror. Good enough to be seen by any standard. She crept downstairs. There wasn't a sound in the front rooms and a quick check revealed Linus had indeed gone out with Mr. George. She grinned. Freedom, however temporary, was sweet.

She hurried to the rear of the house, aiming for the kitchen, where Cook was preparing tonight's meal. Mrs. Baker limped through the room awkwardly, her foot bound firmly following an accident with a kitchen knife.

"Your foot will never get better at this rate," Julia cried out.

"It is better already thanks to you." Mrs. Baker smiled. "I've just got to get my work done, dearie."

No matter how much Julia protested that the foot must be rested, Mrs. Baker refused to neglect her duties in the kitchen.

"Sneaking out again?" Mrs. Baker asked, eyeing the shawl she clutched.

"I cannot bear this prison a moment longer." Julia smiled

brightly. "I'm only going as far as the Watsons' house. I want to see Imogen and ask how her eyesight fares today."

"No doubt the same as it was yesterday, and all of the days of the months before that." Cook shook her finger and then winced. "'Tis a miracle, that's what it is, and you shouldn't go looking to see every day if it has been reversed."

"I agree." Julia nodded as she grasped the door handle. "But I will use any excuse to call on a friend again."

Cook was sympathetic to her situation and had even once allowed her to hide in the larder when Linus had been at her all day. Linus did not want anyone to see her misbehaving again for fear of setting everyone else against her. Given his unreasonable restrictions, she had no choice but to make good use of the rear door or windows of her home to sneak into her friend's house from the opposite direction he'd gone.

Mrs. Baker wiped her hands on a cloth. "He wants the best for you."

"Shouting at me isn't going to change anything," Julia grumbled.

"No, it won't, but…" She shrugged and returned to her baking without another word. Mrs. Baker held back saying what everyone else had suggested out loud at least once. *A good marriage would restore my reputation.*

Well, she couldn't marry until the right man asked for her hand.

So far, Mr. Anthony Linden had not even tried to kiss her and, according to Lady Imogen Watson, reticence of that kind wasn't good during a courtship. Not that he was courting her. Julia simply hoped he would realize she was in love with him. So far, the man appeared unaware and she had no idea how to hurry the understanding upon him.

She slipped out the back door, holding her shawl tighter around her shoulders. Never before had she worried so much about what other people might say when they saw her, but since her spectacular win against Valentine Merton, she took nothing for granted. She was respectably dressed in a blue-and-white striped muslin gown and for a change her hair was not out of place. She was determined to make a good impression because she never knew when she might see Mr. Linden next.

As always, her gaze strayed toward Valentine Merton's home as she passed his rear boundary. The bachelor had accepted his loss with good grace and even better humor, dumping her back into the churning sea as if she was just another fellow. It had been nice, even if she'd sucked down a lungful of seawater due to her surprise at his treatment. He'd pounded her back and apologized profusely, ensuring she was unharmed and suffered no lasting ill-effects.

But that moment of camaraderie had been replaced by fear for Imogen's health soon after, and once assured their neighbor had recovered her sight, that ease between her and Mr. Merton had never returned.

She paused and listened for sounds within the remnants of an old stable that Mr. Merton had converted for his nightly observation of the star-filled sky. At least that was what she'd been led to believe he did in there. He could be very noisy at times, tapping away on things she didn't understand. Perhaps he was building a new telescope.

She dawdled at bit. While she did not blame him for avoiding them, she did not like that he would.

As if called by her presence, Mr. Merton stepped out of the little shed he used for his astronomy observations, wiping his hands on a scrap of linen. His pale hair was untidy today, and a streak of something dark marred his right cheek. He'd left off his coat, revealing his lanky form.

She smiled, determined to make him realize she did not expect more from him than a simple greeting. "Sir," she said with a respectful dip, mimicking behavior other ladies used around men whose opinions matter. "How goes your study today?"

"Good morning, Miss Radley." He nodded and then hesitated; so clearly, she knew he would make an excuse to go next. "I should be getting back to it."

When he turned away and reentered the old building, Julia, at her wits' end, fumed. What must she do to restore the balance? Forswearing adventure wasn't in her nature but the urge to commit violence on him was growing daily, given his ridiculous behavior.

She completed her journey to Lady Watson's door and chatted with the kind housekeeper as she was led into the sitting room. Imogen, married two months, was shuffling papers on her lap but set them aside to greet her. "I heard him today."

Across from her, Miss Teresa Long hurried to pack away her embroidery.

"The whole of Brighton has heard my brother's rants. If they hadn't thought me a bad example before, they certainly must do now." She plopped down beside Imogen and eyed the papers. "Hello, you two. What are you doing?"

"I have written an account of my lost sight and eventual return for Doctor Hill's records. I thought perhaps my recollections might be of use to others facing an unfamiliar future. It was very hard not to lose hope when the world was black."

Impulsively, Julia embraced her friend. "You were very brave. We all thought so."

"There were some who didn't." Imogen scowled, most likely thinking of one woman in particular who hadn't been at all comforting during Imogen's frightening ordeal. In fact, Melanie Merton had been sent away from Brighton, although most thought her leaving the result of preference rather than banishment.

She glanced across to Miss Long. "Has anyone heard from Melanie?"

Teresa, Melanie Merton's cousin, shook her head so swiftly her blonde ringlets bobbed beside her ears. "I must return home. I promised Val my help. I look forward to seeing you again soon, Lady Watson. Miss Radley."

The woman hurried out, leaving silence in her wake.

"Not one word from Miss Merton for months, and I'm glad." Imogen shook her head. "We were never really her kind of people."

Melanie Merton's "people" consisted of older women, ladies who'd never climb a fence let alone race a man, ladies who would have thrown a fit of vapors at merely a quarter of Julia's physical achievements. The type to stand around and tell other women what to do. Julia hadn't really missed those uncomfortable moments. "It is still strange to be in Brighton without hearing of her, seeing her, or suffering her disappointed stares from morning till night at this time of year."

"We will learn to bear the absence." Imogen sighed and squeezed her hand. "What will you do about your brother?"

"Endure."

Imogen burst out laughing. "Are you not being a trifle melodramatic, my dear?"

"It's all I can do." She sighed and twisted a red curl around her finger and tugged savagely. "Mr. Merton spoke to me on my way here but I could tell he'd rather have ignored me again. That's almost as bad as being shouted at."

Lectured, expected to give up her hoydenish ways and

concentrate on finding a husband. Yes, ignored and avoided was ten times worse than anything her brother had thrown her way.

"It's not as if I was the one to insist he marry me. For heaven's sake, he should know that was all Linus's doing. A clever man like Mr. Valentine Merton would not want me for a wife. The idea must have been mortifying. It is no wonder he avoids me now."

"I had thought better of him too but perhaps he's more like Melanie than we realized."

"I never thought so. He was ten times more fun once." She sighed. "Well, there is no denying I was faster in the water than him. I need a new challenge to set for myself now."

"Another? Oh heaven help us."

Julia patted Imogen's hand soothingly. "Fully dressed, I promise. Next time I will not have to pester the fellow to race me. I have learned my lesson. I will not bother Mr. Merton again. They must want the challenge too."

Imogen smiled. "Perhaps, now the dare is over, Mr. Merton simply doesn't know what to say. Men often don't understand that silence causes more harm than good."

"Linus has never had a problem in expressing his opinions." She stood, suddenly keen to put the past behind her. "However, I think it's high time Mr. Merton and I sorted this out or I shall not bother to look at him again."

"I do not like to see you so upset, and over something that cannot be changed." Imogen gestured toward the window. "Is the sky free of clouds?"

"Yes. Oh!" she exclaimed. Understanding at last how she might just corner Valentine Merton for a private tête-à-tête without her brother, or anyone else, knowing brought a grin to her face. "If the sky is clear of clouds tonight, Mr. Merton will almost certainly be stargazing. He is always alone for that. Oh, Imogen, you are a genius."

"I've heard that before from Abigail." Imogen bit her lip. "Now, make sure no one sees you sneak out to him. I don't think there is any reasonable excuse that can save your reputation from a second scandal, should you be caught alone with him tonight."

"I won't be caught." She grinned, imagining Mr. Merton's ease once their misunderstanding was behind them. "I promise to be on my very best behavior."

Chapter Two

There was nothing more comforting than dining in a home where every breath is accompanied by the ticking of two dozen clocks. When they chimed all at once, the noise deafened. Valentine Merton was accustomed to the racket, being in the habit of keeping the clocks he made in his workshop properly wound at all times. "What do you think of my chances, sir?"

Mr. Faraday, an elderly man with a shock of white hair and failing eyesight, waited until the house was silent again before replying. "Your application has caused quite a stir among the company."

He schooled his features not to show his eagerness at the news. Interest was what he hoped for most, rather than outright dismissal. He was an unusual candidate, without the years of training most possessed, but Faraday had claimed he had a gift and he was determined to grasp this chance to make a change in his life for the better. "How so?"

Mr. Faraday slipped his glasses on and then picked up a pocket watch left on the table, Valentine's latest creation. He turned the piece over in his hands, inspecting every aspect. He brought the watch very close to his face so his failing eyesight could make out the finer detail. "You have accomplished much on your own, sir. An item such as this will no doubt delight the eventual owner." He set the pocket watch aside and turned his attention to the small ormolu mantel clock next. "Very elegant, sure to be desirable to any home of good taste and distinction. Yes, your customers will love them both and tell all their friends."

The praise reassured him. "I'm very proud of both pieces."

"As you should be." Mr. Faraday removed his glasses and carefully folded them. "My eyes these days are not so good for the finer details required for my career anymore. It is a great disappointment to me not to be able to pursue my profession as earnestly as I once did. As it is, I shall have to close my shop soon."

"The end of a great era," Valentine murmured. The loss of sight could end a career and make one very anxious. Valentine required neither eyeglasses nor magnification for the finer detailed work. He was luckier than most, he'd been told. "I can understand a little of how you must feel."

Faraday set his eyeglasses aside. "How is Lady Watson getting on these days?"

His neighbor had lost her sight, and had it return unexpectedly all at once. "Her eyesight is much improved, sir, and she has been able to resume her correspondence again without any undue strain."

"What do you believe cured her?"

That was the question everyone asked. "I am not sure we will ever know. She had fallen and struck her head that day. The blow appeared an inconsequential matter at first but within an hour she could see shapes and light once more. She experienced pain. I understand she almost did not realize she could see faces again."

"A miracle."

"A fortunate day." Valentine was careful not to make reference to the other event of that same day. His race against Miss Julia Radley had immediately preceded Lady Watson's return to health, and made many uncomfortable when it came up in conversation.

Mrs. Faraday bustled into the room, followed by a manservant bearing a tray of refreshments, and he was grateful for the distraction. Valentine quickly returned the mantel clock to its box but left the pocket watch out on show.

"I took the liberty of arranging tea. Mr. Faraday cannot tolerate spirits so close to midnight." Mrs. Faraday beamed at her husband as she passed over a strong cup of tea and then spared Valentine a careful glance. "It has been good to see you again, Mr. Merton. It's been too long since you came to dinner."

"Forgive me." Valentine had been keeping a low profile on purpose. He'd quickly grown weary of the jabs about his loss against Julia Radley, and then in the next breath having to listen to insinuations that Miss Radley was *fast* outside of the sea, too, which couldn't be further from the truth. "I trust your children are well."

"Oh, yes. Edgar is much the same of course. Quite busy with his growing family but I do wish he'd visit more often. My daughter's become very popular of late and mentioned just the other day how much she misses seeing your sister about town."

At the mention of his sister, Valentine inwardly groaned. Everyone outside of his friends asked about Melanie but few understood the real reason for her departure. He'd sent her away to keep the peace. "I had a letter from her today and she is quite busy in Oxford. I fear my father has stolen her away from us for some time to come."

Mrs. Faraday appeared genuinely disappointed, as many Brighton matrons were when he broke the news. "That is a great pity. She was such a strident voice against young ladies who foolishly flouted the conventions required by greater society."

Strident? Opinionated. Cutting. At times without any trace of tact. Melanie had offended many young women with her words. Especially his friends' sisters.

Even so, Valentine missed his sister. She had been the most painfully honest person in his life. Having been the one to insist she return home to their parents for a time was a decision he had agonized over ever since.

He toyed with the pocket watch before passing it over when Mrs. Faraday showed interest.

"A lovely piece, sir," she murmured. "Reminds me of the first piece Mr. Faraday made for me when we became engaged. I carry it in my reticule every time I go out."

He inclined his head and met Mr. Faraday's keen gaze. "Do

you think my application to join the company will be accepted?"

Faraday studied his teacup. "That is unclear. The company does not adopt many craftsmen in a year and your situation is different than most. Acceptance depends on more than just skill."

"Oh?"

"Strong family support is vital to all members."

A chill swept through Valentine at this unexpected emphasis. He'd worked hard to hone his chosen craft but his parents had no idea his hobby had grown to mean so much to him. Father would not approve of his decision to apply to the Worshipful Company of Clockmakers either. The man believed trade was beneath them and expected Valentine to take up a teaching position at the Radcliffe Observatory, Oxford, before too long. Mama would likely fall into a swoon at his impending loss of status.

"A stable and prosperous situation in society is preferred, too," Faraday murmured. "What affects one affects us all."

Gooseflesh raced over his skin. "I have lived in Brighton for most of my life. I am well known about Town."

Faraday arched a brow. "Hmm, perhaps too well known, and for the wrong reasons at present."

Valentine broke out in a cold sweat. "You are speaking of the race, are you not?"

"I am attempting to warn you that such indiscretions will not be tolerated or dismissed so easily." Faraday glanced at his wife. "The company has a reputation to uphold. Being defeated by a slip of a girl is less than pleasing to many of the members."

He glanced at Mrs. Faraday too. The woman was examining her fingers and would not meet his gaze. He had hoped for a sign from her that the matter was not so serious as to ruin his chances entirely.

"Miss Radley is a strong swimmer," he assured them. He refused to use the word "fast" for the obvious twist everyone seemed to place upon it.

Mr. Faraday grunted. "She should be ashamed of herself."

Valentine stared hard at Faraday, on the brink of being uncivil. "It was a fair race. Nothing more scandalous than that I assure you."

"Still. It doesn't set a good example for you to have been

involved," he warned. "The company will meet to discuss your application next week. I shall let you know the outcome either way."

Faraday stood and held out his hand for Valentine to shake. The sudden dismissal had a ring of finality to it he did not like. Would Valentine be denied his wish to obtain their support for his work just because he accepted and lost a challenge?

She'd been a worthy opponent and he'd done his best. He'd not been able to match her zeal and catch her that day.

He tucked his mantel clock under his arm and reached for the pocket watch Mrs. Faraday toyed with. When he took it, Mrs. Faraday climbed to her feet. She followed him toward the front door while her husband remained behind sipping his tea.

Once in the hallway, she glanced behind them and then drew close. "The company really only admits married men to their ranks, or those soon to be married."

The whispered warning came as a shock. "I've never once heard that before."

She winced. "It is not really a secret. Most craftsmen do marry young, and your behavior with Miss Julia Radley worries my husband greatly. He supported your application to join the company as a bachelor because of your skill and connections. But even so, with the scandal, I must tell you he has met with considerable resistance."

"I see. I have no plans to marry." His craft consumed his every waking moment, which made the time required to pursue a lady to marry a great inconvenience at present. "What else can I do to win their good opinion?"

"If your sister had remained in Brighton, the situation might not be so problematic. Her sudden departure makes it appear she disapproves of what you've done." She grasped his arm. "Without her presence to win the company over completely, then you must propose marriage to Miss Radley as soon as possible."

"We have only ever been good neighbors. I hardly know her. I will not marry a woman just to suit the company. It is not right." Valentine's heart pounded. It wasn't the first time someone had suggested he must marry Julia to wipe away the scandal of the contest. It was, however, the first time anyone had suggested that marrying Julia might be in his own best interests. "I thank you for your candor, Mrs. Faraday. Good evening."

"Good luck, sir." She eased the door shut behind him.

Outside, a dense fog had crept over Brighton, and knowing his home so well, he made his way to Cavendish Place without deviation, cursing under his breath. He would not tie himself to Julia just to improve his own situation. She was too young, too excitable for the quiet and serious life he wished to live. She wasn't interested in him as a man either, except to use as a method of proving a woman could be as fast and as strong. In that alone were their goals aligned. He had been proud of her achievement, even if her success was entirely unconventional.

He let himself into his home and sighed. No, marriage to Julia wouldn't suit either of their temperaments or needs.

"Valentine?" The query spun him about.

His cousin, Teresa Long, stood on the stairs, her hand to her throat, her dark-blonde hair down and falling over one shoulder. She had stayed behind in Brighton when his sister had returned to the family. The sea air was better for Teresa's constitution than anywhere else and she made few demands on his time, save for the occasional request of an escort to an entertainment with friends.

He removed his hat and hung it beside the door. "What are you still doing up, cousin? I told you I would be late home tonight."

"I couldn't sleep. The house is always too quiet when you go out. I could not bear to close my eyes until you came home again."

Teresa had revealed a startling timidity since his sister had gone away—small things that had previously escaped his notice seemed to set her nerves on edge. She started at strange creaks the house made from time to time. Waking him when she believed she'd heard a knock at the door or a window rattle. When he went out to his workshop, she usually visited him once a night just because she imagined a shadow from the window. Hiding what he was doing out there had proved a difficulty. Melanie's absence had changed Teresa, and not in a way he could accept.

"I'm sorry Melanie is not here to soothe you when I'm about my business. I regret having to send her away, especially tonight." She might have helped him decide what to do next.

"I'm sure you had very good reasons for your decision. She assures me in her letters that she is quite content in Oxford. You don't have to worry about her anymore." Teresa smiled. "You seem troubled, Valentine. You can confide in me as well as you could in her. We are almost brother and sister. You can tell me anything and I'd never betray you."

"Thank you." Only Melanie understood the true reason behind his desire in applying to the company for membership and become a businessman. He wished more than anything in his life to get out from under the yoke of his parents' expectations. He needed his independence, and going into trade would secure that. Melanie understood their restrictive conventions wore him down more every year.

However, he'd never once revealed his ambitions to go into trade to his cousin, and he hesitated to tell her now. "Well, I'm home. Off to bed with you."

She drew close and smiled up at him. As was their habit, he extended his cheek and her lips brushed against his skin lightly. "Good night, Val."

"Pleasant dreams."

She crept upstairs slowly, nightgown and robe lifted above her ankles and clear of the treads. Valentine averted his eyes and, when her bedchamber door rattled, he made his way outside to his workshop for another few hours of toil. He glanced up as he crossed the yard. The fog had drifted away and it would be a fine night for stargazing if the activity still suited his interests. He hadn't touched a telescope in over a year, not since he'd promised himself he'd go into business as a clockmaker.

As he approached the door, he couldn't mistake the glow of light around the doorframe, and grew alarmed. An intruder? He picked up a garden spade from beside the vegetable patch and cautiously pushed on the door.

He glanced around, looking for signs of life.

A slender figure, outlined by the glow of a candle, rose from his workbench chair. "Good evening, Mr. Merton."

He knew that voice very well, unfortunately, and dropped the spade to hurry inside. "Miss Radley?"

She moved toward him eagerly but Valentine took a step backward to keep a distance between them. "How did you get in here, and why?"

"The key is easy to find and I thought you'd be stargazing tonight. I was going to look at the stars while I waited but I cannot see a telescope anywhere."

"You wouldn't see a thing in the sky with the lamp lit," he warned her. "You'll have to go."

She set her hands to her hips. "For the last time, it was only a race. Hardly scandalous. You do not need to avoid me like I am diseased. Can we not be friends again?"

"We cannot ever be friends."

"That's ridiculous. We have always been friends." Her eyes narrowed. "Or have you only been my brother's friend and merely tolerated my company?"

"It is not that." He hated to hurt her feelings but the truth was best. "Simply put, the more we are seen together, the more talk will be stirred up. To be found together and alone is disastrous. The talk would not be kind to you."

The hurt in her eyes took his breath away. Julia had never learned to school her emotions. What she felt was written all over her face for anyone to read.

"So it is true what they say. You are embarrassed to have lost to me." She covered her mouth with one hand, and then squared her shoulders. Her eyes lost their usual mischievous sparkle. "It must batter your pride to have lost to a female as foolish as I," she accused him in a voice tinged with anger.

He caught her arms before her voice grew any louder and eased her toward the door, intending to push her out. He did not want them to be caught together, alone in his workshop. Not after all the terrible things said about her around town. Not after listening to her brother rant and rage every single day for the past three months. "Stop right there and we can talk tomorrow."

She tried to shake off his grip. "Tomorrow you will ignore me again and I've had enough of that."

The best thing for her was to go. He pushed her harder

toward the door.

In the candlelight, her eyes widened and she resisted him. "I thought you were a gentleman. Unhand me!"

"I'm not in the mood for misunderstandings, Miss Radley. You simply must leave."

Her hands lifted to curl about his biceps and squeeze. The discomfort her digging fingers inflicted was a surprise. Julia was stronger than he'd expected—and then *he* was the one being moved. They wrestled for dominance a moment but unless he wanted to risk hurting her, they were reasonably matched. He took a breath. "Why do you provoke me?"

"I'm not." And yet she did not let go of his arms. "I don't believe that because you are a man, you must be obeyed at all times. Linus is just as overbearing."

"I'm nothing like Linus and you know it." Frustrated by her obstinacy, he jerked her against him.

Julia landed against his chest, her fingers pinched into his arms as she stared up at him.

Her lips parted in surprise. "Valentine?"

"Must you always be so bloody stubborn?"

"But we're not done speaking." Her eyes flashed with fire again, the same spark of life and excitement that had convinced him to accept her dare.

He nudged the door shut with his foot instead of throwing her out and pressed her back against the door. "God help us both if my cousin spots us together."

"Teresa would say nothing about it once I explained why I am here."

"Why *are* you here? You know what people will say about us if we are found." As he stared at her, a sudden urge to bend her to his will overtook him. She was wild, and a firm hand could tame her. The idea took hold as he stared into her glorious green eyes.

Could the reason she pursued him like this be that she'd grown to like him?

There had been a time he'd wondered about her. One summer she'd fluttered her eyelashes at him in a dazzling manner that might have meant she had a spec of dirt in her eye, but later he'd realized could have meant something entirely different. She'd not behaved in that manner since but perhaps she'd just been shy. After the race, he *had* held her to ease her distress over Imogen. He convinced himself he'd merely offered brotherly comfort.

But I've never held my own sister that way.

With Julia so close now, he had a perfect opportunity to discover the state of her heart and his own.

He leaned forward, aiming to brush his lips across hers.

They touched; a delicate brush that sent his pulse racing. *Yes!*

Then, faster than he could think, she took his feet out from under him and he fell hard to the workshop floor.

Valentine groaned and remained where he landed, a blush climbing his cheeks.

He had not known she could topple a man, but given how strong she had proved to be, he should have expected he'd be rebuffed. "What was that for?"

She stood over him, hands on her hips. "Don't you dare try to change the subject."

"I wasn't. It occurred to me tonight that there might be another reason you keep smiling at me so often."

She glared. "I want you and my brother to be friends again."

"I can do without a friend who acts and speaks as he does. But you are an entirely different matter." He made himself comfortable, shoving aside a scrap of discarded timber that was digging into his aching backside. As much as he'd like to make another attempt to steal a proper kiss, he conceded he was probably safer where he was sitting for the moment. "You've come to see me alone, at night, and think yourself my equal. Perhaps we should be in all things. You know what people will assume."

"They can assume anything they like. We know what happened."

He scratched his head. *That kiss.* That brief kiss had affected him indeed. "I think we have but one choice—and I *dare you* to marry me to prevent any further scandal."

Her eyes rounded and she threw his workshop apron hard at his head.

His last sight of Julia was a pair of lean calves as she hitched up her skirts to run back home.

Chapter Three

<hr>

Julia glanced about the foreshore, noticing the attention her presence caused. Some men were staring at her, some turned away. The women were whispering again, trying not at all to hide the fact that she was the topic under discussion between them. The gap between approval and disgust was palpable. She smiled up at Anthony Linden and hoped he didn't notice or pay any attention to her detractors. "Would you care to join us for a stroll?"

The corners of Anthony's mouth turned down. "If only I had the leisure, I would be very happy to accompany you *all*. However, I'm to meet with a friend to discuss an expedition. We mean to conquer Scafell Pike next summer."

"So you *are* going to the Lakes District? How wonderful." The possibilities of the expedition were endless and Julia stepped forward eagerly. Adventure, achievement. The challenge of success. "I meant to tell you earlier that we have old friends who live not far from there. I will write to them immediately and give them the good news to expect a visit."

"It's a dangerous undertaking," Imogen cautioned.

Anthony beamed, his eyes filled with zeal and excitement. "What good is a challenge that isn't even attempted, Lady Watson? We fellows are a determined lot."

Imogen lightly grasped Julia's hand and tugged. The subtle pressure to step back from Anthony was clear but she evaded her friend. "Indeed, yes."

Sir Peter Watson grinned. "And who is joining you on this madcap expedition?"

Julia held her breath. Linus was fit enough to go with them if he could be convinced the adventure was worth the time. If Linus went, she would surely earn an invitation to join them, since she'd be properly chaperoned in her brother's company. She could just see herself, scaling the heights, enjoying the clearest views in England with Anthony Linden at her side. It would be wonderful to get away from Brighton and her detractors.

"Oh, the usual fellows, I expect." Anthony swept his dark locks from his eyes. "Johnson, Gallen, Neal. I'm of a mind to invite Merton. Fellow adventurers."

Her stomach dropped at the mention of Valentine Merton. She'd been trying not to think of him, and his ridiculous suggestion that they should marry, all day.

"No women in your party?" Sir Peter asked, his brow rising to reveal his surprise.

"Far too dangerous for any woman." Anthony shook his head, his eyes far away. "But I'm sure we'll need some help with packing provisions and such. There's always so much to be done."

Sir Peter's eyes narrowed and he glanced at her with an expression loaded with regret as she struggled with her disappointment. "Yes, women are such expert organizers," he agreed.

Imogen rolled her eyes. "Have a care, husband."

"You know my views well, darling. There is none more capable than a woman in any endeavor."

Imogen was lucky that she'd married a man of sense. Sir Peter had never spoken dismissively of any woman, to Julia's knowledge. He was unfailingly open-minded about many things and a great deal of fun.

Anthony turned to Julia, unconcerned by the debate he'd sparked between the Watsons. "If you could write to your friends and give them my particulars, I would be forever in your debt. Damned expensive undertaking. I'd like to discuss the expedition with them and see how they might help us secure lodgings and supplies."

Julia winced. Why would Anthony relegate her to the role of helper when she wanted to be intimately involved? She'd thrown out so many suggestions over the past month as he'd shared his dream of conquering the mount. Anthony had lapped them all up and praised her too. "Yes, of course."

"Excellent. Now, if you'll excuse me, I have an expedition to captain." Anthony took his leave, offering a jaunty wave as he went.

Julia watched him go, at once envious and savagely disappointed. Being overlooked stung, and she'd been overlooked a lot in her life. If she'd been born a man, her invitation would have been assured. "I will never understand the way the world is run. If I had a say, *I'd* be captaining that expedition instead of staying behind."

"One day, you will go," Imogen soothed with a quick glance at her husband. "We cannot have everything we want all at once."

"I see." Julia had thought she had already made allowances for Anthony Linden. She'd known he would need time to accept her strength and courage was a match to his. Her ambitions were just as valid and important as anyone's. Perhaps it was a failing of all men to dismiss what they didn't understand.

Valentine Merton might be an exception, although she wasn't so sure she would ever understand him entirely. He would be excited about the expedition; to see the stars from a closer perspective would be a lure for him too.

"I wish I had been born a man."

"I'm glad you were not." Sir Peter frowned. "If you were a man, I'd never allow you to be so close a friend to my wife. I'm quite possessive of whom she keeps company with. As all men of romantic persuasions are, I must warn you."

Imogen caught her eye. "Is there a particular gentleman responsible for that scowl? Your brother, perhaps?"

"Linus could not be worse."

"Then what? Did that meeting we discussed yesterday occur last night?"

"Yes." Out of the corner of her eye, she saw Sir Peter smother a grin. Imogen had warned her that she and her husband kept no secrets from each other. Clearly, she'd told him everything about her intentions to visit Valentine last night. If only the evening had made things easier. Instead, it had been a waste of time. She wished Sir Peter hadn't known. Last night had been so embarrassing.

"And?" Imogen almost shook her. "Do I have to drag every small detail out of you? I've been waiting nigh on an hour for an accounting."

"He proposed and I knocked him down," she confessed quickly so the humiliation was over as soon as possible. Julia clenched her jaw. She'd been too shocked to think like a lady last night and had defended her own honor in the only way she could. Knocking Valentine to the ground might have been rude, but she'd never suspected he'd consider she'd welcome a proposal, or a kiss.

If she had even considered her visit would prompt that kind of response, she'd never have bothered. Julia certainly didn't think of him in that sense...not romantically. She would not even contemplate his ridiculous suggestion that they marry. She was only trying to mend the breach in a friendship. He must be mad or foxed to have uttered the insane proposal.

"Was that your way of accepting?" Sir Peter asked, eyes twinkling.

Julia scowled at his amusement. "No, of course I did not accept. He hardly meant it. What sane person goes around daring a lady to marry them?"

"What woman goes around daring men?" Sir Peter asked, giving her a pointed look to remind her she *was* that woman. "He was unusually quiet early this morning. I assume he was disappointed with your mode of refusal."

Julia hadn't exactly said she refused but her actions should have proved to him how unwelcome his advances had been. "I am not happy with him either. He tried to kiss me."

The baronet grinned. "Why are you angry about that?"

"Have you lost your mind? I could not ever be Mr. Merton's wife."

"What's wrong with Val?" Sir Peter appeared confused. "He's

a decent sort, plump in the pocket enough to afford a wife and not entirely bad to look at."

None of that was untrue. "Oh, please. Of course you'd list his positive qualities only. You're his friend."

"His *best* friend," Sir Peter insisted. "I think he would make a very good husband. Very loyal."

"Hounds are loyal." Julia scowled and met Imogen's gaze. Behind her, Sir Peter continued to grin broadly. *Blasted man.* "I won't marry him. I won't even speak to him again until he comes to his senses and behaves normally. I may not speak to your husband again, either, if he doesn't stop smiling."

Imogen gave her husband a nudge. "Go away. You're upsetting her and making things worse."

In response, Sir Peter kissed his wife's cheek and then strolled ahead toward an orange seller's stall without another word. "I'm sorry. He's growing worse every day. Always on the lookout for a match to be made. Such a tragic romantic."

"You know how I feel on the subject of marriage."

"Yes, it is very hard to miss your infatuation with Mr. Linden has not waned." Imogen resumed a slow walking pace. "To be truthful, and I know you don't want to hear my opinion again about him, but, I don't believe he's possessed of reciprocal feelings for you. Maybe you should consider Mr. Merton's proposal. He is a good man."

"Anthony is wonderful," Julia insisted. Mr. Linden had been everything she'd ever wanted since she could remember. A skilled athlete himself, he told such fascinating stories of his travels and successes. She couldn't wait to be part of that world and go away with him. She would insist upon accompanying him everywhere once they were married.

"But Valentine was the one who accepted your dare when no one else would." Imogen linked their arms and walked on. "Mr. Linden is just a touch too sure of his appeal, don't you think?"

Julia tossed her head. "People are often jealous about another's success or popularity."

"Sometimes." Imogen shrugged. "I simply wish he'd spend more time listening to you than talking about himself. Anyone could see you wanted to go with him, which reminds me to warn you again about wearing your heart on your sleeve in public."

"We will never agree on this," Julia insisted. "I don't care who knows how highly I regard Mr. Linden. I love him."

Imogen sighed deeply. "One day, perhaps you'll understand the difference between infatuation and real love."

Julia turned away from Imogen without a word as Sir Peter returned juggling three oranges for his wife's amusement. Of course she understood what real love felt like. She loved Anthony with her whole heart. When they were together, it was as if nothing else existed but him.

She was certain she could eventually bring Anthony up to scratch. She just needed to be patient. Some married couples were so sweet together. Take Mr. and Mrs. Faraday, who were approaching, arm in arm. Mr. Faraday tended toward gruff speech but his wife was entirely devoted to him. They'd been married for thirty years and were forever in each other's pockets. When Mrs. Faraday glanced up at her husband, she saw nothing else.

Especially not the hurried approach of a rough-looking man who snatched her reticule from her grasp and hurried away with it before the woman could even cry out in protest.

Julia grabbed two oranges from Sir Peter, sighted her target, and flung the first fruit, catching the man a glancing blow to the shoulder. His stride broke but he didn't fall, so Julia chased after him a few steps and flung the next. She landed a solid hit to his back and he fell.

Thankfully the man lost his grip on Mrs. Faraday's reticule as he regained his feet with a vile curse and then fled the scene empty-handed.

Sir Peter, who'd also given chase, stopped at the nearest corner crossing and glanced around. "Damn, lost him," he called back.

Julia hurried for Mrs. Faraday's reticule, and after brushing off the lovely silk accessory, quickly returned it to the distraught woman. "Are you all right? I hope nothing of value is damaged, Mrs. Faraday."

"Thank you. Oh, that was such a fright." Mrs. Faraday stared at her as she held her reticule close to her chest. She blinked back tears. "How did you do that?"

She shrugged. "Practice and good aim. The first shot went wide because I wasn't concentrating hard enough."

Mr. Faraday set his arm about his wife's shoulders and squinted at her despite his glasses. "Who are you?"

"Miss Julia Radley, sir. I know you both by reputation, of course. My brother patronizes your shop when our clock needs repair. A pleasure to make your acquaintance."

However, her stomach flipped when the man turned away from her immediately. "We should go home."

Most of the older set condemned her now, and despite her good deed, it seemed they still would. However, she did not regret her behavior today. She had acted on instinct, even in an unladylike manner, and despite the likely lecture coming from Linus she would do it all again. Her behavior had aided another. "I hope you are unharmed, Mrs. Faraday."

Mrs. Faraday glanced at her wrist and rubbed over it. "A little abused but…"

"May I?" At her nod, Julia carefully peeled back the lady's glove and inspected the reddened skin around her wrist. "Cloths dipped in a strong violet-leaf tea, after cooling of course, soon and repeated before bed. I would not embroider or sew for several days to allow proper healing if I were you. If it pains you greatly when bumped, perhaps a binding of linen, firmly done, would offer support for the hand and wrist."

Faraday peered at her strangely. "You have experience with injuries of this nature."

"Only my own. I once tripped and twisted my ankle very badly on a long walk. I was some distance from home and by the time I returned, my ankle had swollen from overuse. I could not walk freely for several days."

"I see." Faraday glanced down at his wife. "I'd better get you home, my dear."

"Thank you, Miss Radley." Mrs. Faraday touched her arm. "I truly appreciate what you did for me today."

They turned for home and a small crowd of older residents went with them, asking question and offering aid. She smiled at how Mr. Faraday ushered his wife along with one arm wrapped protectively around her back. Old people were so sweet, even when they didn't entirely approve of her.

Imogen clutched her arm. "That was amazing. I had no idea your aim was so true."

"It normally isn't, but I suppose I had the proper incentive. Mr. and Mrs. Faraday looked so happy moments before the thief struck." She sighed. "I think I was a little angry that their mood would be spoiled."

"Well, whatever the reason," Imogen gave her a quick squeeze, "no one could fault you for thwarting a thief. Not even Miss Merton could complain. She's an intimate friend of the Faradays, if you remember. So is Mr. Merton."

Julia sighed. By nightfall, Valentine would certainly be regretting his rash marriage proposal to someone like her at that news.

"Val dined with them last night," Sir Peter added. "I thought he was courting the daughter, but after what you told us of his proposal, I'm not so sure that could be the case. He's not one to act rashly."

"Well, this will prove his mistake." Julia dusted off her gloves and straightened her shoulders. "I'll not stand in his way if he wants Miss Faraday. She would undoubtedly be better for him."

Imogen nodded slowly. "Perhaps you are wise to be cautious. Reading between the lines from what Teresa Long has confided over the years, Melanie is sure to cause trouble in Valentine's marriage, especially if she doesn't approve of the wife."

Julia shivered. Melanie presented two faces to the world—a proper lady every matron over forty adored, and the critical schemer, utterly vicious in private. She'd do anything to avoid a confrontation with her. "She certainly would."

Chapter Four

"I cannot believe she told you I proposed, and after she turned me down flat." Valentine dropped into a generously padded chair in his parlor and groaned as pain flared. Being injured was bad enough. Being injured because he'd been an utter dolt and beast in the bargain pained him more. "Does she deliberately want to humiliate me before the whole of Brighton?"

Sir Peter Watson merely smiled. "Judging by her scowl—a match to your own at this moment, by the way—I think your offer offended her sensibilities."

"Offended her? I was trying to do the right thing," he protested. He'd been watching for her all day, undecided on how to act when he did see her though. Mostly he wanted to ask how she'd knocked him down in the first place. She had the making of a worthy wrestling partner if she'd been born a man. "Infuriating minx. I think I should not have bothered to worry for her reputation. She is more than capable of defending herself should there be a need."

"You've had three months to do the right thing with regards to the scandal and didn't. I hardly think a little nighttime visitation called for a marriage proposal, unless you were already considering it." Sir Peter raised a brow. "The real reason, now. Out with it."

Valentine sighed. "We were alone."

Sir Peter grinned. "And?"

"And nothing." Embarrassment filled him. For one brief moment he'd forgotten he was a gentleman and kissed her. If not for her stunningly swift reflexes, he might have done more. He was not proud of his behavior. "I was attempting to do what is right."

"And her response to that was to knock you down?" Peter laughed. "Come now, surely you gave her just cause for that action."

Valentine had so hoped Julia had not shared the events of their whole meeting, but it seemed she'd not been discreet with their friends and had told them everything. "I never so much as touched her."

"Such fibbery." Sir Peter shook his head and grinned. "You tried to kiss her."

A flush of heat filled his face but he wouldn't confirm or deny the accusation.

"She went to see you last night, at Imogen's suggestion I must add, to mend fences so you and Linus could stop avoiding each other." Sir Peter seemed to neither need nor wait for his response. In fact, he seemed delighted by how the evening had ended. "I will offer my congratulations. You have changed her opinion of you, my friend. That is very much in your favor for a positive outcome."

He shifted in his chair to ease the pain of his bruise. "I don't see how."

"The problem with Julia—and all of our sisters, really—is that we were brother figures to them all their lives. We watched over each other's sisters without ever noticing they were growing up before our eyes and I assure you, they did the same to us." He grinned. "You're no longer a man to dismiss as merely her brother's friend now, or opponent. You, my friend, are a prospective suitor at last."

"I *was* her brother's friend. Linus won't even acknowledge me lately."

Sir Peter spread his hands wide. "Marry her and Radley will be reasonable again."

"That is the poorest reason to marry Julia, let alone any woman."

"Then what other reason could there be to propose? You don't love her, do you?"

"I don't." His sudden reversal in opinion, to ask for her hand last night, seemed inexplicable even to him in the cold light of day. A marriage would certainly restore Julia's battered reputation and the company did prefer married men in their ranks. However, neither reason should have been enough to make him blurt out a proposal. He wasn't that shallow a man. He'd thought he'd known his own mind.

When he married, Valentine wanted something warmer than his parents' cold alliance. A woman immune to outside influence would be desirable too. Whether his father approved mattered little if he had his way and went into trade, although he imagined life would be more harmonious if he wed someone the women of his family approved of. Melanie already expected him to marry Julia. She'd railed at him for not seeing the need immediately after the race.

Sir Peter regarded him with a smile. "Well? Why the offer of marriage?"

Indeed why? He'd been affected by her energy last night. The excitement in her eyes as they'd tussled. She had the determination of a man beneath her curves, and that strangely appealed to him more than proper women did. "I like her energy."

"She never does stay still," Sir Peter agreed.

"I don't mean that exactly. My sister says Julia willfully ignores propriety but I don't think that's entirely true." He thought back over the past weeks and years of their acquaintance. "Julia is different to every other woman I know. Louder, impulsive, but never mean-spirited. When I agreed to race against her, she was so feverishly excited that she would at last discover her physical limits. She does understand what's expected of her. She just doesn't want other people's expectations to hold her back, and neither do I. I don't take after my family in that regard."

"Your family could be a problem." Sir Peter slapped his back. "Sounds like you have your work cut out for you. Good luck convincing her to take you on. With parents like yours, and that acid tongue of your sister's in the mix, you might have only a slim chance."

"Was that why she ran from me? Because of my family?" He shook his head, appalled by that suggestion.

"Perhaps in part, but I suspect she really refused because she's infatuated with someone else."

Anthony Linden. He shook his head. "Still? I thought she would have seen through Mr. Linden's overblown accomplishments by now."

Sir Peter appeared surprised. "You knew about that and still asked her to marry you?"

Valentine shrugged, unconcerned with the idea of Julia and Anthony Linden. "I've never believed Linden was at all serious about Julia. Melanie mentioned it ages ago. A terrible match, she termed it."

"Perhaps. She's very interested in Linden's life and his plans. He's undertaking an expedition to conquer Scafell Pike in the summer. Julia wanted to go so very much but Linden mentioned only fellows, you included."

He nodded slowly. She would undoubtedly relish the challenge of a dangerous climb as another means of testing her strength and endurance. "Julia is always drawn to the unusual."

"However would you satisfy her adventurous spirit?"

That was a question he hadn't considered. Julia was not like other women. He couldn't see her being satisfied with the life his sister had been groomed for. His interests in his budding career would keep him in Brighton indefinitely. "I don't know."

"Good answer." Peter slapped his hand down on the table. "It's best to decide these things together anyway. I've learned never to think too far ahead if I want peace at home."

"Interesting. Married a few months and already a master of the subject."

"A student of Imogen," Peter corrected. "And a happy man. I highly recommend you take up a similar study of your own quarry."

"Obviously." Which meant, if he was serious about making Julia his wife, he had to court her properly. Next time Valentine spoke to Julia, he would make sure she understood he admired her tenacity, and long before he attempted another kiss. His backside still hurt and he shifted again. He would find out what she wanted most or die trying. Hopefully his pursuit would not come to such a final end. She hadn't exactly refused him so he would ask again just to be certain.

"So, are you coming?"

Valentine blinked. "Where?"

"The lady under discussion is visiting my wife at this very moment."

Well, that solved the immediate problem of seeing her without appearing overly eager. "If nothing else, I can apologize for last night."

Peter paused at the door and raised one finger. "If I might offer some advice; never apologize for wanting to kiss a woman. She would see it as an insult. Women like to feel irresistible as much as we men do."

Valentine nodded and followed Sir Peter. "So wise, my lord."

His friend snorted. "Don't call me that."

Sir Peter hadn't quite come to grips with his elevation to baronet, and Valentine did enjoy tweaking his nose about it by using his title as often as possible in private.

Teresa met them in the hall, carrying her sewing. "Are you going out again?"

He nodded. "To Sir Peter's home."

Teresa sighed heavily, as she did so often now. It was as if she feared outside that door was another scandal just waiting for him to step into.

For a moment he feared Sir Peter would invite her, but when his friend remained silent, he breathed a sigh of relief. He did not want to begin a courtship with his cousin laughing at him from across the room. "I will try not to be too late," he told her before stepping out and following Sir Peter to his door a few houses down.

Animated laughter filled the Watsons' house, and he smiled as Julia chortled. She did like to laugh a great deal. She was perched beside Imogen, her hands above her head as if she were about to toss a ball. "Charades?"

Her hands dropped as their gazes met. "No."

Imogen nodded to him. "Julia is something of a hero today. She singlehandedly prevented a robbery by the judicious use of two oranges."

"A robbery? Where?"

"On the foreshore. And she wasn't the only hero. I did my part and chased the villain away," Sir Peter complained.

Imogen laughed softly. "And you gave splendid chase, darling, even if you fell far behind in the end."

Valentine sank into a chair across from them and awaited further explanation. Neither lady appeared ruffled by the experience so he concluded no one had been harmed. "What happened?"

Julia shrugged. "A thief snatched a lady's reticule and tried to run off with it."

"So what did you do with the oranges?"

"I threw them." She toyed with her gloves, eyes downcast. "Stunned the man enough with the second that he dropped what he had taken."

"Good grief." He reeled at the danger she'd placed herself in by taking on the attacker. "Thank heavens your early morning exercises found a use."

Julia gave him an odd look. "What do you know of that?"

"How could anyone miss the hours you practice? Tossing balls into hoops, lifting heavy objects, running jumps with your skirts up to your knees when you think no one can see you. You never stop moving." Melanie had kept him appraised of her many indiscretions over the years, and he'd seen enough with his own eyes to glimpse her commitment to testing her limits. Still, attacking assailants was dangerous. "What would you have done if he'd turned around and tried to harm you?"

Her eyes narrowed. "I won't be bullied."

"I wasn't trying to harm you last night," he replied calmly, stopping short of an apology. "But the next thief you meet might turn around and finish what he'd started. Do you know how to defend yourself?"

She licked her lips and cast a nervous glance at the Watsons. "I know enough to best *you*."

"I would not count on it in every situation. Very few gentlemen would teach their sisters this but I have shown Melanie how to protect herself. She refused to believe that such instruction was required and so far that has been the case." He gestured to her. "Stand up."

"Why?"

He stood and took off his coat. "Because if you're going to start attacking the criminal element, you might as well learn to fight like one. I will teach you."

"You're joking?"

"Not at all." He looked around the room. It would have to be here and now. He may never get another chance. "I'd rather not hear that you've been hurt through folly."

Imogen stood, hiding a smile as her husband began to move smaller furniture and trinkets out of the way. When they had a clear space, standing on opposite sides of the carpet, Valentine faced her. Julia appeared skeptical.

"I'm going to grab you."

He lunged without further warning, caught her arm and turned her about so her arm was twisted against her back.

She yelped in surprise and pain. "Valentine!"

He glanced behind him to see if the way was clear. "Now you need to make me release you. One way is to push me back into a wall, hard, in the hopes I'll let go. Do it."

Julia pushed but he resisted with all his strength. He was impressed by her efforts, but not enough to let her win.

"I can't shift you," Julia protested.

Sir Peter folded his arms over his chest, his expression serious as he observed them. "Another way might be to smash your heel into his toes, kick back at his shins, or reach behind to gouge out his eyes."

Valentine loosened his grip immediately before she could enact any of his suggestions and Julia stepped free, rubbing her wrist.

"Do you have any questions?"

"No." She turned away and Valentine grabbed her again, this time winding his arm about her chest. He held her tight against him and, being taller, lifted her feet clear of the floor. She struggled valiantly but her determination was no match for his strength. Even though her fingers dug under his to loosen his grip, he wouldn't give up.

She reached for his face and as soon as her fingertips touched his skin, he jerked his head aside. "If Sir Peter hadn't been there, you might have given chase," he whispered into her ear. "What if the bounder had possessed a knife?"

Her breath caught.

The little fool hadn't thought of her own safety for one moment. "Taking on thieves is dangerous. How will you escape me now?"

He slid his free arm around her waist, completing his hold on her. She wasn't soft or pliant but made of steel. Even so, she was heaven to hold.

The reason behind his sudden proposal snapped into being—he liked women who enjoyed adventurous bed play. Julia might be that sort of woman one day, if she was carefully introduced to the possibilities.

He sucked in a sharp breath, filling his lungs with the scent of honeysuckle as she turned her face as far as she could.

"I don't know," she growled in obvious frustration, then bit her lip. Her lashes fluttered and he was lost.

God help him, despite the watchful company about them, he was growing aroused by her. He fought his response, determined to hide this private side of his nature.

"Think quickly." He placed her feet to the floor.

Julia turned in his arms until she was facing him and before he could jump back, her knee rested against his groin. She balanced on one foot, her hands fisted into his shirtfront.

Her eyes met his, triumphant. Excited. "How about that?"

Valentine pushed her knee away from his privates. Secretly impressed but so glad she'd not maimed him. "If you had used any force at all, your assailant would have been howling in pain."

"Good to know for next time."

Valentine moved closer and splayed his fingers across her hip. "Be careful, minx. Someone is always likely to be stronger than you."

"I know." Her gaze softened and she licked her lip. "Thank

you for the instruction. You're the only one who has ever treated me like one of the fellows."

He stared at her lips. "You haven't the faintest idea of how I think of you."

Julia swallowed.

A throat cleared. Two throats, in fact. Valentine glanced beyond Julia to find both Imogen and Peter hovering at the door. Both appeared uncomfortable and he understood why. He'd promised himself he would not rush into kissing her again, and he wouldn't. But he wanted to very much. That much should be clear to anyone. He stepped back. "I should be going."

Julia's face fell. "So soon?"

He nodded quickly, pleased that she sounded disappointed. "As much as I enjoyed this, I suggest you don't mention today to your brother."

"The less Linus knows the better," she agreed. "As it is, when he hears about the Faraday incident he will undoubtedly be cross again."

"What do the Faradays have to do with you?"

"That's the lady whose reticule was snatched today." She smiled a little sadly. "They were very shocked."

He could also imagine Faraday's pride being bruised because the slip of a girl he'd complained about had rescued his wife's possession. The incident didn't bode well for the man's continued support. "One can only hope his shock remains until Sunday."

"What happens on Sunday?"

"The start or end of my hopes." He bowed to her but didn't elaborate. "Good day, Miss Radley. Sir Peter, Lady Watson. Thank you for an enjoyable afternoon."

Chapter Five

———◆———

Watching other people dance all night was a bore. However, until one was asked, a lady had no choice but to stand on the sidelines. Julia had danced twice, once with Sir Peter, no doubt at his wife's urging, and once with Mr. George, who hadn't seemed his usual cheerful self. No one else had bothered to approach her. It had so far been one of the most mortifying nights of her life.

"Stop fidgeting," Linus whispered out the corner of his mouth.

"I should have stayed at home rather than endure this." At home, she could practice what Valentine had shown her of defending herself instead of watching everyone else have fun. At present, all of their friends were occupied, either dancing together or mingling with Brighton society in a way she no longer could.

"You won't find a husband if you remain unseen," Linus hissed.

The musicians struck up a new tune that had her toe tapping. She wished Anthony Linden would ask her to dance tonight but he twirled about on the dance floor with other women, having the time of his life. "But if I had stayed at home, I wouldn't be whispered about or stared at."

Linus glanced around. "Then make sure they see you at your best."

Her best wasn't what anyone wanted to see, she suspected. Tonight, even the Faradays had given her a wide berth, despite the good she had done for them in thwarting a robbery. It wasn't fair. "I have a headache."

"You do not. We will stay until the last set and walk home with everyone as usual."

"At least I will be among friends then."

Linus grunted. He had been glued to her side all night, making sure she behaved. That didn't stop some gentlemen from smirking at her when he wasn't watching, and she hated that most of all.

Julia clapped along with everyone else when the final set ended but her heart wasn't in the evening. She glanced longingly for the terrace doorway but her gaze landed on Valentine Merton. He stood on the far side of the room, beside his cousin, and appeared to be having a very nice time too. Valentine's cousin was staring at him, her gaze full of warmth…and something she'd never noticed before as he led her to the door to take their leave.

Julia's stomach twisted. She knew that look. It was the same expression Imogen wore when she teased her husband.

Love.

Mortification filled her and she glanced away quickly, sure she had seen something not meant for her eyes. Since the race, Teresa had been cool to her, almost disapproving. She bit her lip and joined everyone else in leaving but there was no escaping her conclusions.

Ahead, Valentine and his cousin strolled along arm in arm. They always did so, now that Melanie was gone from their company. And as she observed their ease with each other, she began to feel sick to her stomach. What was Valentine doing proposing to her when his cousin clearly had feelings for him?

Linus grabbed her arm and tugged. "Keep up."

Valentine glanced over his shoulder and met her gaze. He frowned slightly.

Julia forced a smile and stumbled along, trying to work out how she'd never noticed Teresa's partiality for her cousin before. The woman shared his house. Did Teresa share a deeper intimacy with him, now that Melanie was not there to prevent it?

Imogen dropped back to her side while Sir Peter distracted her brother with plans for tomorrow. "You didn't enjoy yourself tonight?"

"Not particularly." She shook her head to clear it. She should not be thinking of Valentine Merton beyond friendship. "I've never enjoyed being idle for an entire evening. What I need is a really long run if I'm to get any sleep."

Imogen stared ahead. "But you did enjoy tea this afternoon. It seemed as though you thrived on the instruction offered."

She was such a fool. Valentine had no real interest in her if he was loved by Teresa. She would make him a perfectly respectable wife. "I did then." She sighed. "Such an afternoon will never happen again though."

"Are you sure that would be true?" Imogen squeezed her hand. "A certain gentleman seemed very intent on your education. I imagine if you accepted, he would not change, but grow bolder with you."

A flush of warmth filled her cheeks. She *had* enjoyed her time with Valentine. "A whim, I'm sure. Nothing more."

Imogen fell silent. "I am having a great deal of trouble imagining Melanie participating in such instruction."

"Melanie would never raise her knee to a man's groin," she murmured softly. Much less tolerate such a scandalous embrace. "She would have fainted to have seen me with her brother today."

"I shall have to find out if he's instructed Teresa in the same manner."

The idea of Valentine's arms tight around Teresa Long's body made her unreasonably irritated, and she was glad to see her doorway ahead. "No doubt he has," she ground out.

Imogen caught her arm. "Julia, whatever is the matter now?"

"Nothing." She kissed her friend's cheek and forced her annoyance away. "Good night, Imogen."

She fled inside without a backward glance, hurried up to her room and slammed the door shut. Once inside though, she paced her room. There was no way she could sleep tonight, not as restless as she was. Not as confused as she had become.

Valentine and Teresa? It wasn't possible, and yet…

She threw open her window and glanced out into the night. The moon was up, but the patchy clouds offered sufficient cover. A fast sprint up and down the lane in secret should do the trick and rid her mind of her speculation before sleep. Everyone would be going to bed soon and she could be back before her brother even realized.

She stripped off her fine gown to change into a practical one, making sure to secure her brother's old breeches underneath, and then laced up her feet in a pair of sturdy shoes.

After assuring herself her brother was in bed and snoring, she threw her leg over the windowsill and made her escape.

A few feet from the ground, she was grabbed from behind and a warm, bare hand clamped over her mouth.

"Don't scream," Valentine whispered into her ear. "It's me."

She relaxed instantly and was helped down to the ground, although she didn't need the aid. She couldn't see her neighbor clearly with the moon now behind a cloud. When he grabbed her hand and tugged her toward the cover of a tree, she didn't resist. However, he led her to the rear gate and gestured her out. "Ready to run?"

His whispered words sent a thrill through her, even more so when he took a stance that suggested he would race her too.

She nodded and caught the sides of her gown. "Go."

She took off, not in the direction of the lane but toward the ocean, and a safe path to travel far on foot. The ground flew beneath her, accompanied by the pounding of Valentine's feet at her back. She grinned. This was far better than dancing. Intensely exhilarating. Liberating in a way she'd never experienced before.

When she judged she had run far enough, she slowed to a stop and caught her breath.

Valentine caught her arm and swung her about in a circle. In the moonlight, he was grinning. "I thought you'd never stop."

She glanced back toward home, a faint spec in the distance, and grinned too. "I didn't realize we'd gone so far."

Valentine pressed his free hand to his chest, gasping still. "You put most fellows to shame. Myself included."

She grinned. "You kept up well enough."

"I had the incentive of chasing you." He tugged her toward him. "Try not to hurt me this time."

"Why?"

"Because I need to kiss you." He dipped his head and his lips brushed hers softly. "I'd follow you anywhere you wanted to go, too." His arms closed around her body as he deepened the kiss.

She couldn't move for the shock of Valentine wanting to kiss her again. Hadn't she proved just how much of a hoyden she was?

And yet, he was still kissing her. Making little noises and tugging her near. She resisted and he groaned. Another thrill. Unexpected longing filled her and to her surprise, she discovered kissing him was too good to halt.

Julia clung to his arms. The novelty of their race, the thrill of the chase, had excited her and after a moment of indecision, she wound her arms around his neck and returned his feverish kisses. Her feet left the ground and he moved them from the path, into a spot protected from the ocean breeze, where he held her close against him.

He drew back. "Gods, you are exciting, minx."

He wasn't so bad either. The way he slowly nibbled at her neck sent gooseflesh all over her skin. "How did you know I wanted to run?"

He cupped her face, his thumbs brushing over her hot cheeks. "You didn't dance more than twice tonight. You seemed uncomfortable and I just knew you'd find a way to exert yourself. I didn't want you in danger."

He slipped his hands low around her hips and drew back. "You're wearing breeches?"

Julia nodded, waiting for criticism.

Instead of suggesting she should not, or that she was foolish, Valentine stroked down her legs and back up to her waist. He groaned. "*That* I will have to see for myself one day."

Julia pushed against his chest, and glanced toward their homes anxiously. She wouldn't show Valentine anything she didn't want to. She wasn't that sort of woman. She wore breeches to preserve her modesty and because they were an incredibly practical garment. She had no wish to be ruined just because she dared to dress differently to other women. "Walk or run?"

"Walk." He caught her hand with a smile, once more a friend and not a seducer. "That will give us a chance to talk."

"What is there to talk about?"

"Marriage."

Julia wrenched her hand free and stumbled forward a few steps before finding her voice. "Why would you want to marry me?"

"Because of tonight, and this afternoon at the Watsons, and our race."

"You're worried about how people regard you." She nodded. "I won't tell anyone about tonight, or this afternoon. The Watsons would never tell."

"I'm not concerned for myself, but for you." He smiled softly. "I find myself wondering how much more you could achieve if you had support."

"What I want has never seemed to matter very much at all." Julia rubbed her arms, disturbed by how she longed for the support Valentine mentioned so casually. Linus may never accept her nature, and Anthony Linden hadn't noticed how she longed for adventure. She had to face facts—she might never reach her goals. "You should be more concerned for yourself."

"Oh, my dreams are small." He curled her arm through his. "I wanted to open a shop actually, here in Brighton, but I'd rather you not spread the word about that venture now, if you don't mind."

Julia snorted. "Are you afraid your sister would not approve of you going into trade?"

"My sister was my confidant and something of a silent partner in the scheme for the past two years," Valentine insisted as he dragged her along.

"She was?" Julia couldn't hide her surprise.

"My parents, however, would never approve, and so I haven't told them or anyone else. They think I tinker with telescopes but I've discreetly sold a dozen or more clocks this past year through acquaintances and distant shops. Opening a legitimate premises of my own was to be the next step."

Was there anything this man couldn't do? "And of course you will."

"That remains to be seen."

"Why?"

"In part because of us." He patted her hand soothingly. "Also, apparently, I need to marry or be on the brink of marriage to have won over the company of clockmakers for admittance. Without their approval I would have a very difficult time getting underway. I hadn't known about that requirement for marriage until this week, in fact."

"So when you asked me to marry you it was to appease them." She stared at him in horror. "That's a terrible reason to propose to me."

"That wasn't why I asked you." He shrugged. "I like you, as if you couldn't tell tonight by the way we kissed, but it is true that everything I want is in jeopardy. No matter what I do, they will make the decision by the weekend and that will be that."

"What happens if you don't open a shop?"

"My future may not involve a comfortable life." He made a face. "My father has been at me for years to follow in his footsteps and take up a career in Oxford. He believes he holds the purse strings but he doesn't realize the extent of my independence. I would do anything at all, muck out stables if necessary, rather than return to live beneath his roof again."

"I understand." Julia's life depended on Linus, and when she married, she'd march to her husband's drum. "I'm sorry."

"So what do you think?" He stopped and turned her to face him. "Do you accept my challenge? Do you dare to marry me?"

Valentine had been distant, almost cold sometimes. Except when they were alone, as they were now. She folded her arms over her chest and glared at him. "You snubbed me in public."

"I have not." He suddenly turned sheepish. "Well, I haven't *exactly* snubbed you. I have been polite and made sure our meetings never had a hint of impropriety attached to them, but you keep seeking me out. I don't think you realize how badly people have spoken of you behind your back. That is why Linus is so angry with both of us. I thought it better to keep a distance than feed the fire of gossip."

Julia kicked a pebble in her path. "Linus says I brought it on myself."

"I was right there beside you on that beach and haven't endured half of the criticism. It isn't fair to you." He unfolded her arms and caught her hand in his. "I do not regret our race but the consequences for both of us were greater than I ever imagined. I am only sorry for that."

"What about Teresa?" she asked in a choked voice. The way he stared at her, touched her, was rather overwhelming but she had to know how he felt about Teresa once and for all.

He frowned. "Teresa must live with us. The sea air is best for her health and she will be company for you when I am occupied elsewhere."

Her tension eased only a little. Much like her, Teresa had feelings for someone who didn't see they existed—which made what she'd been doing with Valentine come into stark relief.

Would she ever have allowed Anthony to kiss her as Valentine had done without an understanding? She didn't think so. She felt different with Valentine. Alive and unguarded. "What will you be doing elsewhere?"

"I will be making a living, constructing clocks or mending them." He grinned down at her. "Melanie tells me it is incredibly boring, watching me at work on something so tiny she needs eyeglasses to see the detail, so I thought to spare you too."

Dear God, she had forgotten all about Valentine's sister. Melanie would not be pleased by his intention to marry her. "And what of Melanie? Will she come back?"

At that, Valentine stopped and stared out to sea. "I don't know. I miss my sister very much. I know many do not like her, I suspect no one misses her, but she has smoothed my way on many occasions, and I do wish she was here now. I could use her advice."

"About marrying me?"

He shook his head and grazed his knuckle over her cheek. "About this unexpected turn with the company."

"What does Teresa say to do?"

"Teresa does not know what I want for my life. I have not confided in her. She is very close to my parents." He shrugged. "I don't believe she would approve, actually, and I'm not sure she wouldn't try to talk me out of my plans."

"I see." Julia bit her lip, confused by his thinking. "But you've told *me*."

"If you are to be my wife, then there should not be any secrets between us or unpleasant surprises for you. You need to know that you're not marrying an idle fop." His lips lifted into a wide grin. "I trust you and you can trust me. Tell me about Anthony Linden."

Julia blushed. "I don't know what you mean."

"Are you in love with him?"

"That is a very personal question, sir."

"I suppose it is, but can you blame me for wanting to know how you feel about him?"

Julia bit her lip and turned away. "I don't know now how I feel about anything."

"Is it simply the lure of his expedition or has he expressed affection for you?" Valentine moved to stand beside her. "He'd be mad not to fall for you, you know. You're funny, charming, athletic."

"Everything a proper woman isn't," Julia murmured.

He shrugged. "Proper has its time and place. If I hadn't been improper with you, I'd never know so much about you now."

"Such as?"

He caught her hand. "You smell of honeysuckle, you laugh and fight with your whole heart. You are quick-witted and very, very strong. You may be unconventional compared to other women but there is nothing unattractive about your interests."

"Oh," Julia whispered as a blush climbed her cheeks at the compliments. Thankfully the moon was behind the clouds now and Valentine couldn't see how his words affected her. Those had been the nicest compliments she'd ever received. No one usually liked that she wasn't the same as everyone else. "Thank you."

"When I'm with you, I want to challenge you," Valentine continued.

Julia glanced behind them. "You have. I've never run so far from home before alone."

"We raced together. We could do a great many things together that challenge us both if you were my wife." He kissed her, cupping her skull, and despite everything she'd assumed, she leaned into him for more.

He eased back and met her gaze. His hair was tousled by the breeze, pointing up at all angles, and he appeared unbelievably handsome to her suddenly. She couldn't believe he still wanted to marry her and she glanced down to hide her reaction.

He caught her chin gently and raised her face again. "What do you want from me, Julia?"

"Nothing." Julia shook her head, fighting the blush burning her cheeks at the direction her thoughts were taking her. "But I don't mind kissing you."

"I will court you properly. Your brother will expect it." He kissed her soundly and then glanced toward their homes. "We have to go back."

"True."

He dug into his waistcoat pocket. "That reminds me. I have something for you. A token of my esteem and admiration."

He handed over a gentleman's silver pocket watch and she frowned at the unusual item. She held it until the moon shone strong again. It was beautiful; the heavy chain attached to it was cold silk in her fingers. "My brother would not approve of me accepting any gifts from you."

"It's not for him to know about if you don't want him to yet." Valentine turned the piece over, showing her the face.

In the moonlight, it seemed quite lovely, but she could not make out all the details. "Did you make this?"

"I did." He nodded. "I hoped you might find a use for it in timing your daily exercise."

"I..." Julia choked up and covered her mouth with trembling

fingers. Valentine was too generous. She blinked back tears. "I've always wanted one but Linus refused."

"Hmm, I suppose Linus would see it as encouraging your tendencies for the unusual. Do you like it?" When she nodded, he closed the face. "I can hold on to it until our wedding day if you'd rather not provoke him."

Although she longed to keep it, she pushed his hands back. "He has been difficult enough as it is."

Valentine kissed her temple. "No longer. Not if you marry me."

Julia hesitated. It was every young lady's dream to catch the attention of a man who took her interests seriously. By the sound of it, she had ruined Valentine's plans and yet he still wanted to marry her. He was getting a very bad bargain indeed. She didn't know if that made him a fool or incredibly optimistic.

He did kiss nicely though, and he did know her a lot better than she'd ever suspected. She felt a pang of longing for Anthony Linden but then pushed that hope aside. Not even he had offered to test his strength or skill against hers. Only the man standing before her, offering his name to mend her reputation gave her hope for a better, challenging future.

Valentine, despite their differences or perhaps because of them, was willing to accept the way she was and that pleased her. She'd be a fool to turn down his generous offer, especially after the manner in which she'd spurned the first. "I will. I will marry you."

She wasn't sure what she had expected after her answer but when Valentine swept her off her feet and spun her about until they were both gasping with laughter, she clung to him tightly. He kissed her hard on the mouth and then drew her toward home. "Next time I propose, try to appear surprised for your brother's sake, and whatever you do, don't knock me down. A proposal shouldn't turn into a wrestling match, no matter how appealing the idea might be to both of us."

Her eyes widened. "You would wrestle with me like you would with a man?"

He grabbed her and pulled her close. "Definitely."

A thrill shot through her whole body at the dark tone behind his words. Perhaps she really had made a good choice—but there was still Melanie to contend with. She wasn't looking forward to seeing Valentine's family again.

Chapter Six

———◆———

Valentine shook Linus Radley's hand. "The banns will be read on Sunday. I'll go now to speak with Mr. Pease and begin arrangements immediately."

Radley raked his hand through his hair. "Thank you. This has been a difficult time for the family."

They were standing in Linus Radley's study, a place he'd not visited in many, many weeks. The room hadn't changed but circumstances had. He was uncomfortable here now. The last time he'd stood in this room, Radley had insisted that his only option had been to marry the man's sister. Considering he was about to do that very thing, marry Julia, he would be very pleased to escape the reminder. Of course, now he was marrying Julia entirely because he wanted to, and because he thought they would be good together.

Like last time, Radley didn't seem to care what Julia thought about marriage.

He was not at all concerned about Julia's happiness in this arrangement. He just wanted the scandal to be over and her married off to anyone who would take her. Valentine found Radley's attitude offensive and unreasonably cold. "Thanks are hardly required, but you have mine for entrusting me with her happiness."

"She could not have done better," Linus replied.

Was that a compliment or an insult? He stood uncomfortably, unsure how to respond, and then shrugged off the feeling.

The terms of settlement had been discussed and agreed upon. There was nothing left to do but wait and say their vows. Given the time that had passed since the race and ensuing scandal, Linus had been eager to complete everything today and he'd been brisk and efficient. "Let me show you to the door."

"I should like to say goodbye to your sister, if I may."

Radley frowned but gestured toward the parlor, where Valentine had left Julia after going down on one knee and proposing properly. "If you think it necessary."

"I do indeed." He was eager to see her again. As agreed, they shared no references to his first proposal. He was especially grateful, because the first had ended with him dumped on his backside. Radley could become angry with Julia if he should find out about that. He'd bellowed at her more than enough over the past months for Valentine's liking. Now that she would be his wife, he was determined to put a stop to the daily harassment.

He caught Julia's eyes as soon as he entered the parlor and smiled warmly. She had been all fidgety nerves on his first arrival and she still seemed anxious even now. "All settled."

Linus Radley paused at his side. "Mr. Merton is leaving."

Her face fell. "Already."

"I'll see you soon." Her disappointment touched him and he strode across the room and caught her fingers gently in his. "I'm just on my way to see Mr. Pease."

A worried frown crossed her brow. "Good luck."

"None required." He touched the fingers of his free hand to her pocket watch hidden in his waistcoat, just to remind her that he carried it and would be thinking of her.

"Mr. Merton," Radley called from the doorway.

Valentine ignored the impatient man in favor of stealing a few moments more with his intended bride. "I hope you have a pleasant day, Miss Radley. I'll be counting the minutes until I see you again."

He brought her hand to his mouth and kissed the back of her glove. "Everything will be better now," he whispered. "I swear it."

"Thank you, Mr. Merton."

"That's enough of that," Radley warned as he stepped between them.

The light in Julia's eyes dimmed a little. Undeterred, by Linus's rudeness, he smiled warmly at her. "We are engaged to be married, Radley. There is nothing improper about kissing the back of her glove."

A muscle in Radley's jaw ticked. "I don't care what you do after the wedding. Until then you will keep a respectable distance."

Valentine kept his annoyance in check. Radley really had become a stuffed shirt about propriety in the last months. He wasn't sure he liked this change in his character but he had no wish to argue today. "As you wish."

Reluctantly he took his leave of Julia, but he'd have rather stayed behind and talked a while longer.

"Enjoy your day, sir," Julia called softly as he reached the door.

He turned back with a smile that promised he'd see her again soon. Julia knew he would go through the motions of what a suitor was required to be in public. In private though, he would be himself with her. He hoped in the meantime Julia could curb her impulses and appease her brother. He hoped she never got caught sneaking out the window or back door to talk to him in the weeks ahead.

On the street, he paused on the footpath as a fine black carriage swept past him and then he crossed the street. He didn't feel his marriage would influence the company in his favor but as every moment passed, he was even more certain it was the right thing to do. Especially when Julia smiled at him.

When the carriage that had just passed him stopped before his home, a chill swept over his body and he stopped. He turned slowly as a groom jumped down and put down the steps. When his father emerged on the footpath, his palms grew clammy with shock.

The old man never left Oxford without reason, and his expression was not encouraging.

"No. Not now," Valentine groaned. "Not yet."

He smoothed his waistcoat and moved toward his front door

to offer a welcome, just as his sister Melanie emerged from the carriage. He hurried to her and extended his hand, so pleased to see her again. "Mellie."

She didn't smile, but cast her eyes toward their parent immediately.

Valentine turned his attention to their father immediately at her subtle suggestion. "Sir, what an unexpected surprise to see you in Brighton."

The long, hard stare his father directed at him, rather than a greeting, didn't bode well and Valentine fought the urge to fidget. When his butler opened the front door to welcome his guests, his father rudely pushed past into Valentine's home and strode toward his study without uttering a word.

"Don't keep him waiting," Melanie warned in a trembling voice. "He is angry almost beyond reason. We have not stopped since we left Oxford."

He caught her elbow when she seemed to sway. "You are exhausted."

"Don't worry about me. Worry about him and what he will do next." She pushed him toward the house but despite her warning, Valentine escorted his sister to the doorway and into their butler's safe keeping. Her usual maid scurried after, wearing a worried frown. He turned then and spoke to the large coachman, asking him to wait. The man scowled and Valentine dug into his pocket for coin.

"Thank you, sir." The coachman grinned warmly then as he tucked the money into his mud-splattered waistcoat pocket and then steadied his team, apparently perfectly happy to wait now he'd been paid.

Valentine took a deep breath. To his left, Walter George had stepped onto his front doorstep to see who had arrived, and to his right the Radley's were peeking at him around the doorframe. He couldn't delay another moment to speak with them.

He swept into his home, tossing his hat aside carelessly, noting Melanie had curled into her favorite chair in the parlor and was rubbing her eyes. "Bring my sister tea and a warm blanket as soon as you can," he said to Forbes.

"With pleasure, sir." The older man smiled, turning toward

Melanie eagerly. He left her to his butler's fussing and approached his study door.

His father had planted himself at the window, hands behind his back, feet wide apart. The stance of a man intending on delivering a long lecture. Valentine closed the door behind him to ensure privacy.

"Did you think to fool your mother and me?" his father asked suddenly. "Did you believe we wouldn't hear about your intentions?"

"No, sir." He was aware that news of his behavior would reach Oxford, but at the moment he wasn't sure precisely which bit of news the old man was referring to: the race with Julia or going into trade. Either one his father might complain about. He sent up silent thanks that he couldn't possibly know about the marriage yet.

"You will pack your things and return to Oxford immediately," his father ground out, still without turning. "Once there, you will apologize to your mother for the distress you've caused her. Caused all of us."

Valentine took a breath to steady his own temper. "I will not."

His father spun around. "You dare to defy me, boy?"

It was well past time to stand up to his father. He was four and twenty now and had long past seen a reason to kowtow to his father's demands. "I have no interest in returning to Oxford, not now nor in the future. I made my home here long ago and I intend to stay."

Few men disagreed with his father. By the way his skin mottled red, his temper was still unused to disappointment in the almost year since they'd seen each other. Christmas last year had been a tense affair.

"If you open a *shop*, I will cut you off without a penny," he warned.

Valentine relaxed a bit. At least now he knew what they were arguing about. "As you have threatened before on many occasions when I did not act according to your liking. I will have my way in this no matter what you say."

"Do you think so? Foolish, selfish boy." His father's eyes narrowed to hard slits. "And what of your sister and your cousin?

Do you not think of how your decisions lower their esteem in other people's eyes?"

Always one to tug on his emotions but never to reveal any of his own beside contempt, his father was not above manipulation to have his way. Melanie knew what changes would come by his going into trade and was prepared for every eventuality. Teresa did not know yet but she would fare as well as Melanie, and she'd always have his protection. Mother would have yet another reason to bemoan her wayward son. "I am sure they will survive."

"You stun me with your arrogance."

"I am my father's son," Valentine replied calmly.

His father waved a hand. "Get out. I cannot look at you until you talk sense."

His complacency vanished. He was sick and tired of his father's tone and it was time to lay down a few rules. "This house is mine. Bought and paid for from the inheritance my uncle left to me. You can leave any time you want to, but I will not be sent scurrying just because you demand it."

The old man spluttered. "How dare you speak to me in that tone."

"What would you prefer?" Valentine folded his arms across his chest. "You're looking well father; the semester has been kind to your health."

His father snorted at the attempted pleasantries. The old man hated that kind of talk, which was probably why his parents avoided each other like the very plague. Mother could speak of the weather for thirty minutes without pause. He'd timed her once.

"Very well." He stormed out of the room, yelling as he went, "Daughter. Miss Long. You will attend me at once."

The ladies scrambled to follow him out onto the street and the carriage door shut before Valentine had a chance to speak to Melanie again. They drove off immediately, turning into the heart of Brighton. He assumed his father would return tomorrow to launch a second assault.

George reached his side first. "Where have they gone?"

"The Old Ship, I expect," he murmured quietly.

The Radleys joined him.

"He disapproves?" Julia asked in a tone that hinted she was worried.

"Of the shop, not the other." He caught her fingers lightly, ignoring the surprise on his friends' faces. He hadn't told them about the shop as yet. "I did not have a chance to mention anything else."

She clung to him a moment then let go, blushing furiously. "What will you do?"

"What I'd planned to." He stepped back inside to collect his hat from Forbes. "Visit Mr. Pease and arrange our marriage."

George glanced between them and slowly grinned. "Are congratulations in order?"

Valentine nodded. "Most assuredly. Julia has consented to be my wife."

George slapped him on the back and then shook Julia's hand. "Good. I couldn't have borne any more long faces around here. While you see Pease, I'll discover for certain where your father and sister are staying."

"Thank you, George, but I don't wish to trouble you."

George shook his head stubbornly. "It's no bother at all. I could use the exercise of a long walk this afternoon."

He turned away quickly.

"George is a very odd fellow at times to be chasing after your family," Linus Radley mused. "Always sticking his nose into other people's business. Come along, Julia. I imagine we will be seeing much more of the Mertons, and very soon."

Hopefully they'd not have to endure his family for long or she might cry off. Valentine hurried for the vicarage to prevent that.

Chapter Seven

———◆———

When Julia came face-to-face with the Mertons the next day in Valentine's parlor, her heart clattered wildly. She remained glued to her brother's side, and he seemed to sense the tension around them too. Mr. Merton Senior, Teresa Long and Melanie stood before them unsmiling.

Frankly, Julia was terrified of this intimidating trio, but then remembered there were worse scenarios to come. Enduring Mrs. Merton's exalted presence.

She smiled at the group, attempting to make a good impression. Teresa stood close to Mr. Merton, but she smiled only at Linus. Julia looked to Melanie next. The woman's appearance gave her pause; there were dark smudges beneath her eyes that never used to be there when she'd lived in Brighton. She appeared ready to wilt, which wasn't in her nature at all. Julia was concerned enough to single her out. "Good morning, Miss Merton."

"Good morning." Melanie's expression was a polite mask that showed no pleasure or disgust in seeing Julia and she turned to Mr. Merton Senior immediately. "Father, do you remember the Radleys? This is Mr. Linus Radley and his younger sister, Miss Julia Radley."

Mr. Merton Senior had always scared her, with his barking

voice and his scorn of Brighton's more relaxed lifestyle. Her reaction to him hadn't changed in the years since his last visit. To think he would be her family one day soon made her doubt her decision to accept Valentine.

"Yes, this fellow does look somewhat familiar," Mr. Merton murmured before extending his hand to Linus.

The way he greeted Linus, polite but utterly dismissive, hinted he had no idea she'd soon be part of his family. Julia rated no more than a fleeting glace from him. "How do you do."

Valentine shifted to her side and curled her arm about his possessively. "Father, I have such happy news. Miss Julia Radley consented to be my wife yesterday. The banns will be read on Sunday."

Mr. Merton's gaze sharpened on her. His jaw clenched. His face darkened to a furious shade of red. "Is that so?"

Teresa flinched at his tone, but the most interesting reaction came from Melanie. She bit her lip, glanced down at her hands a moment but when she lifted her face, she broke out in a rare smile. She seemed overcome with emotion. "Congratulations, I hope you will both be very happy together."

Valentine returned the smile. "We will be."

"Thank you," Julia said quickly, relieved the news had been so well received by Melanie. Her acceptance was a positive. Far more than she'd hoped for. For Valentine's sake, she wanted to be at peace with the woman, rather than at odds.

"Have you lost what little sense you have left?" Mr. Merton asked bluntly as he took a step toward his son.

Julia shivered in Valentine's embrace.

Teresa clucked her tongue. "Valentine, this is too generous, even for you."

Valentine frowned at his cousin, confusion clear in his expression, but then he gestured to the chairs. "Please be seated," he murmured, smiling at her and Linus as if his family's reaction was of no surprise. "I had hoped you'd be pleased I was ready to settle down at last."

Julia took a seat beside Valentine and he grasped her hand firmly. "Everything has been arranged for the marriage."

"Surely there is still time," Mr. Merton insisted, shooting

Teresa Long a hard look.

The woman smiled warmly at Valentine. "There is no need to sacrifice yourself."

"What the devil are you talking about?" Linus asked, his voice taking on a hard edge.

Mr. Merton waved his hand. "We can still end this arrangement before any harm is done."

Julia gaped. She'd imagined some disapproval but having it voiced to her face, before her brother, hadn't ever entered her head. She pressed her lips together to keep her protest in. Both Mr. Merton and Teresa spoke as if she could be easily discarded. As if the agreement to marry Valentine was utterly impossible.

She met Melanie's gaze to see if Valentine's sister would now retract her good wishes in the face of different opinions.

Valentine's sister nodded slowly and then she jerked her chin up in a familiar way. Julia understood Melanie's silent admonishment to act as a lady despite what was said around her.

Julia took comfort in the familiar entreaty and managed to smile at Mr. Merton. She would not be persuaded to change her mind, not after discovering Valentine had already lost so much respect on her account.

"It is too late, Father," Melanie murmured, breaking the tension. "If Valentine has spoken with the vicar then the whole of Brighton will have known of the match before sunset that day. He is a shocking gossip."

That wasn't precisely true, although the man did like the sound of his own voice. She breathed a sigh of relief when no one appeared ready to contradict Melanie.

Mr. Merton Senior raked Julia with a furious glance. "Reparations can be made."

"No," Melanie warned. "Julia's reputation would never recover from the scandal of a broken engagement at this point. That situation would tarnish our name too."

Mr. Merton sized her up, and it wasn't a pleasant sensation. "I'd like to speak to her alone."

Linus sat forward. "I beg your pardon? I cannot allow such a thing."

"If you believe I will allow any sort of female marry my son and heir, you are out of your mind, sir. I know what is said about her behavior." The pair glared at each other. Linus was the first to look away. "I want to see the truth of her character for myself."

"I'll stay," Melanie advised them suddenly. When Valentine protested, Melanie threw an apologetic glance toward her father and cousin. "Miss Radley is a lady and must be chaperoned. I will stay with her so the proprieties are observed."

It was a flimsy excuse at best but Julia nodded. She couldn't avoid a discussion with Mr. Merton forever and she'd frankly be relieved for any company when it did happen. She wouldn't like to speak to him alone when he had so clearly set his heart against her. Even with Melanie present as chaperone, she would still feel overwhelmed, but she might prevent Julia from getting flustered. She drew herself up straight, mimicking Melanie's mannerisms for all she was worth. "I'd be very happy to speak with Mr. Merton with his daughter as chaperone."

Although Mr. Merton appeared not to like the idea, he nodded sharply. Valentine, Linus and Teresa left. She could tell Valentine didn't want to leave by the way he kept glancing back until the door closed. Teresa, again, only had eyes for Valentine, and that broke her heart. He clearly had no idea the woman was so enamored of him.

When the door closed behind them, Julia folded her hands in her lap and waited with as much patience as she could muster.

Mr. Merton dug in his pocket and tossed a soft leather pouch at her. She caught it easily. "I'm sure you understand what that is for?"

Puzzled by the weight, Julia tugged on the strings and peered inside. Her mouth grew dry at the sight. Money—more money than she'd ever touched before. "Indeed I do not."

Mr. Merton stood and began to pace behind the settee Melanie was sitting on. The woman appeared to shrink a little. "My son has a bright future ahead in Oxford. He has the education and breeding to excel at anything he sets his mind to and his mother and I have high expectations for him. I have allowed him to play here in Brighton, but no more." Mr. Merton set his hands behind his back and faced her. "I'm sure any damage done to your reputation will be recovered with an increase in your fortune."

Julia cast a glance in Melanie's direction desperately, but Valentine's sister remained silent, her eyes downcast. She would get no additional aid from that quarter in refuting his claim. The idea of being bribed made her furious. "You think you know what's best for me? You barely know my name, let alone my character."

"Women like you come and go. You'll be just the same as the others."

She shared a glance with Melanie at last, one that conveyed he spoke the truth, and a hot blush crept up her cheeks. "What others?"

Mr. Merton ignored her question. "Do yourself a favor and leave my son alone to live the life he was born for, or you will live to regret it."

Valentine had his own ideas for his future, and when he had spoken of Oxford, it had been clear that he didn't want the life his parents expected. Her pride stung her enough to anger on Valentine's behalf. She knew what it was like to be forced into an ill-fitting role. "I believe I understand you."

She understood him, but Mr. Merton had no power to make her obey.

"Good." He strode out, slamming the door behind him. The front door slammed too, and in the next moment, Valentine burst into the parlor. "What on earth did he say?"

Julia swallowed and hid the bribe beneath the folds of her skirt quickly. "That he disapproves of me. That is all."

"I am sorry." He sagged. "I thought he would be this way. I had intended to inform my parents after the fact of our marriage, rather than before, to delay such a conversation."

Julia blushed. So he'd gone against his father's wishes and proposed to someone his family considered unsuitable? Her temper rose. She wanted to throw something, and yet to do so would prove Mr. Merton correct about her unsuitability to join his family. She had to calm herself, and quickly. "Could you give me a moment?"

Valentine frowned. "Yes, of course. Melanie?"

"We both need a moment, brother. This won't take long.

Please."

"Very well," Valentine agreed slowly.

Julia bolted to her feet as soon as the door shut, somewhat relieved that Melanie had stayed. She had lots of questions to answer. "How could he speak to me this way? To anyone?"

She scowled at the money Mr. Merton had tossed, left behind when she rose. It mocked her. She felt herself finally to be as tainted as everyone suggested. She felt ill. Unclean.

"Our father has all the subtlety of an axe," Melanie apologized, her tone matter-of-fact. "Our parents believe happiness and ambition can be achieved through money alone. They will do their best to make your association with Valentine into a sordid affair, too. Father will paint you as a grasping adventuress intent on elevation through cunning."

Julia rounded on Melanie. "And you didn't say a word in my defense?"

"What would speaking up have accomplished? He's my father and I'm dependent on his good will to keep a roof over my head. He does not change his mind. Ever."

"Then why did you insist on chaperoning me?"

"I stayed to witness the truth for myself." Melanie stared at the money. "What are you going to do with it?"

"I can't take it."

Melanie sighed. "You already have, in his eyes."

"I'll toss it into the street."

Melanie patted the cushion beside her. "What will that achieve? A boon for someone else but no resolution."

"Well, I shall not keep it." She threw herself into the space beside Melanie and scowled at the money across from them. "What other women was he referring to?"

Melanie leaned close, pitching her voice low. "I'm afraid he has done this before. Father was particularly pleased with himself about that and spoke of it one night after he'd been in his cups. There was a girl my brother must have fancied himself in love with years ago, the daughter of a custodian at the university, I think she was. He was young and when my parents discovered her existence, they convinced her to go away. Valentine purchased this house from our father soon after, citing a fondness for our grandparents as the sole reason. He suspects interference in many aspects of his life, but this is the first proof I've seen with my own eyes."

"Then I cannot give Valentine the money without upsetting him. I cannot tell anyone."

"Probably not, but such a confession is likely unavoidable." Melanie collected the pouch and after sitting again peered inside. Her eyes widened considerably then she pulled the drawstrings tight. "You cannot hide such a sum of money from my brother if you are serious in your intent to become his wife."

Julia didn't know what to do with the money. She should tell Valentine she'd been tricked into taking it but wouldn't that make her seem dim-witted? "Have you spoken with him yet? With Valentine?"

Melanie sighed and rubbed her temple. "I've not had a moment to myself since we arrived for socializing with him. Father is very demanding. I'm surprised he didn't order me to follow him when he left, but Miss Long is offering an ample distraction with her flattery, so..."

Julia had noticed the way Mr. Merton ordered everyone about. To endure that daily must be a terrible strain. "Then you will need to speak to Valentine today before your father prevents private speech. The company has thrown up an unforeseen obstacle in your brother's path. The vote is very soon."

Melanie expression turned to one of surprise. "He told you of his plans to go into trade and you would still marry him?"

"How could I deny him his greatest wish when he granted mine in our race? He wants to make clocks for a living." Julia nodded. She accepted his decision easily. It was what he wanted most and she would be a supportive wife. "But he said our race had greater implications for his application than he had foreseen."

Melanie nodded and dropped the pouch on Julia's lap. "I feared as much. At least marrying you will soothe some ruffled feathers. You will have to set a better example from now on if he is to win back favor."

Julia shivered and turned the leather pouch over in her hands. She didn't want the funds for herself, but she wanted Valentine to have his wishes come true. She would try to improve her reputation for his sake. She held the money out to Melanie. "I'm damned no matter what I do. Would you mind keeping this for me? If an appropriate use comes to light that could aid your brother, then all the better."

Melanie's expression turned skeptical. "Are you sure you mean that? There is a lot of coin in there."

"What use have I for money? Money doesn't buy happiness."

"Comfort but not happiness," Melanie agreed. She slipped the pouch into her reticle and drew the strings tight. "Now, we'd better speak to my brother and then I must return to my father. Valentine will undoubtedly be concerned about the subject of our private talk. What should I say to him?"

"Nothing as yet. Tell him we spoke of Oxford and Brighton events." She squeezed Melanie's hand briefly, glad to have an ally. "He's missed you and mentioned how much he wished for your opinions."

"And I missed him." Melanie glanced around them. "And home."

Melanie stood and approached the door, clutching her overstuffed reticule tight to her side. Julia followed, hoping the increase in bulk wasn't noticed by anyone. Melanie would have a hard time explaining how and why she carried so many funds on her person.

Julia gathered her courage, plastered on her bravest face and prepared to convince her betrothed that all was well. But deep down, she was sickened by Mr. Merton's assumption that money would get rid of her.

She never backed down from a challenge or dare. She would prove to all that she was a perfectly acceptable choice as Valentine's wife.

He rushed forward and took her hands in his as soon as he saw her. "What happened?"

"Nothing." Behind Valentine, her brother and Mr. George were waiting too. "I merely wanted a private word with your sister. It's been so long since we've spoken."

Valentine frowned. "And is everything discussed now?"

"Yes, but she must speak with you alone." Julia almost stretched up to kiss his cheek but at the last moment settled for a smile. She had to be more like Melanie from now on. "I will speak to you later, yes?"

"Come for dinner, Merton," Linus interrupted. "Bring your sister if she's of a mind to join us."

"I'd be happy to." Valentine smiled. "What do you think, Melanie?"

Melanie shook her head. "I should like to join you very much but our father has engaged me elsewhere this evening. My time is not my own now and I would not be permitted to change my plans."

"That is a shame." Julia sighed, genuinely disappointed to miss a chance to speak with Melanie again. She had been unusually supportive. So different from the past. "Well then, just us three."

Valentine nodded but his expression was puzzled. Regardless, Julia took her leave, and when she was at home and alone once more in her locked room, she settled into a fighter's stance, arms upraised, fists clenched. She'd never been made to feel so cheap before, and only Melanie's sympathy had revealed how normal that result was when dealing with Mr. Merton Senior.

She threw out her fist and snapped it back, mimicking a boxer she'd once seen practicing. She didn't know how Melanie could bear living with parents like that. She threw another punch, and another. Mr. Merton deserved to be taken down a peg or two.

Julia straightened. "There may be no way to fight a man who believes he knows what's right for his son, but I will prove to him I'm no detriment to Valentine's life."

Chapter Eight

---◆---

"What was that all about?" Valentine asked of Melanie after the Radley's had abruptly taken their leave. Something unpleasant had just happened and he didn't like being left in the dark or lied to.

"A female discussion," she murmured.

Melanie paled even further and he checked his frustration. She wasn't well, and looked it. "When did you sleep properly last?"

She shrugged and cast a nervous glance at George. "I don't remember. Might we talk in private, Valentine?"

Melanie often suffered nightmares, a terror she wouldn't name. Judging by the dark circles under her eyes, the dreams had returned, and frequently. "Very well. Go to my study." He turned to his friend. "I'll be with you in a moment, George, unless you'd prefer not to wait."

George's attention remained on Melanie as she slipped away. "I'll wait."

Valentine followed his sister into his study and closed the door. "What did you say to her? Did you upset her?"

"Father had already done his work very well on that score." She gripped her reticule tightly. "Julia needed reassurance."

He couldn't help but be surprised by her claim. Julia was

almost overconfident most of the time. "Reassurance from you?"

Melanie nodded. "As you know, our father is rather abrupt when he speaks to others, especially to women he hasn't a high opinion of. He made certain insinuations against her that were most unpleasant to listen to. She took them to heart initially."

Valentine gritted his teeth. "I'll kill him."

"Don't bother." Melanie shook her head swiftly. "Julia isn't about to fall to pieces because he doesn't care for the alliance and told her so. She's not made of feathers or paper; she's not so easily destroyed."

"She was upset."

Melanie shrugged. "She's had a shock. In the past, most censure has been subtle."

Valentine raked his fingers through his hair. "And Father couldn't be subtle."

"No. She will survive his disapproval quite well, brother. She is as strong of character as I've ever complained of. But her heart is large enough to put it behind her if given enough time." Melanie met his gaze. "Now, forgive me for being in a rush but Julia mentioned you were having some other difficulties and wanted to talk to me. Something to do with the company?"

He gestured her toward a chair. "I have found out that the company requires their members to be married or on the brink of it."

"To make clocks?" Her eyes widened as she sank down. "High-handed indeed to leave it till the last moment to bring it up."

"An unwritten rule, it seems. There is more. Even if I am now to be married, some noses are out of joint on account of the race with Julia. It seems no matter what I do, my ambitions might come to naught."

"I did try to warn you that others would not approve. However, I believed you'd receive nothing more than a warning and that would be that. Men usually can get away with so much more than a woman."

He sighed. "It meant so much to her."

The corner of Melanie's mouth lifted in a smile. "You indulged her."

"And I will keep indulging her. We raced on foot two nights ago when we both couldn't sleep. She beat me again, but not by very much."

Melanie scowled. "So, your known race is but the first adventure you will share? That will not go over well if word gets out."

"If I am to keep her happy, then most assuredly it must be so. I do not mind. She is strong, physically strong, and more than a little determined to avoid the label of wilting wallflower. It's refreshing, actually. She's not the least bit delicate, like our cousin."

He could be himself with her and not have to worry she would faint from shock.

Melanie bit her lip and moved away to the window. "She will turn heads. You both will."

"After the past months of listening to whispers and innuendo, I suspect that will always be the case."

Melanie nodded and drew the curtain aside and peered into the rear yard, where the gardens were. She sighed softly. "An unconventional match will be difficult for many to accept. You will have to win the town over, and how that affects your standing, and the eventual success of your shop, becomes terribly uncertain."

"I know."

"Difficult but not impossible." Melanie turned slowly, nodding to herself. "The work of a lifetime. You must acknowledge the right people, make sure to curry favor with those who matter."

He'd been doing that all his life. "Will Father make trouble for us?"

Melanie nodded. "He's already started. Dinner last night was with the Prescotts and he expressed concern over your choice of friends. He claimed even Walter George to be a bad influence, which as we both know is an utterly ridiculous suggestion to make. Mrs. Prescott and I never had a chance to converse alone but we shared a look, and I believe her unconvinced by father's complaints so far."

"So now that I've announced our marriage, and he so clearly

disapproves, he will likely start slandering the Radleys as a means of tarnishing the match." Valentine gritted his teeth a moment at how bad it could get. His father would try to turn the whole town against them to get his way, just so he would see a future in Oxford as a better choice. That was why Valentine had kept his plans to himself from the beginning.

What Father had forgotten was how greatly Melanie's opinion mattered to the elder townsfolk. Since she'd already accepted his decision to marry Julia, they might turn things around yet. "Can you help Julia? Discourage the worst assumptions Father provokes?"

"While I am here, I will do what I can. We—Father, Teresa and I—have been invited to dine with the Lowes tonight and I will see how the wind blows with Mrs. Lowe. That particular lady speaks her mind no matter who is around," Melanie warned. "Tomorrow, if you would collect me at eleven o'clock, I should like to make some calls. Better not to have Father or Teresa with us for them."

"Why not Teresa? And what is the matter with her?"

Melanie frowned and returned to her chair. Her expression was troubled. "I suspect Father chose to return to Brighton on the strength of Teresa's last letter to our parents. I never did mention the race to him in the end, or express my view that you should have married Julia because of it. I gave what you said to me last a great deal of thought. I am too judgmental. I am far too much like our mother. I have no right to criticize anyone and I apologize for embarrassing you."

Valentine gripped her hand tight. "I missed you."

"But the way Father spoke to Teresa last night hinted they shared an aversion to your plans to go into trade. Her letters to Mother must have contained some hint of it. His decision to come here was sudden and he was furious when he announced his intention to visit to me. I was interrogated for most of the journey here, particularly about Mr. and Mrs. Faradays' characters." She swallowed.

"He also knew about the scandal with Julia, particularly a midnight meeting, although he didn't mention her by name. None of your correspondence to me even hinted you had changed your mind about her so when I learned of it, I was surprised, and very pleased."

"Teresa wouldn't go to Father behind my back." He shook his head, unable to believe such a situation. "She wouldn't intentionally hurt Julia."

"Are you really so naïve?" Melanie frowned, her expression deeply worried. "She is certainly in Mother and Father's pocket. The only other source close to you, who might know of any secret meeting late at night, would have been your nearest neighbors. I doubt any of your friends would have interfered. It's not in their natures to thwart a romantic pursuit in favor of propriety. Think hard, brother, what is to gain if the match does not go ahead, your dreams ended."

Valentine cursed under his breath. His friends were anything but prudes when it came to affairs of the heart. They all knew how he felt about Oxford. "Father wins and he thinks I have no choice but to return to Oxford in disgrace."

And he had distanced himself from Julia until very recently, so no one should have imagined a private meeting could take place. But Julia had shared their meeting with Sir Peter Watson and wife. He couldn't credit either one with writing to his father after all the shenanigans that pair had got up to before their marriage.

Had Teresa been watching him and writing to his parents behind his back? She had written several letters earlier in the week to Oxford. He'd never thought to wonder what she might be writing about. "I thought I had been careful enough not to taint her reputation any more than I had."

"Clearly not enough, if someone wrote and warned them. You do realize they are still currying favor with the chancellor."

Valentine gaped then snapped his mouth shut. "I'm not going to marry that man's daughter. Not. Ever," he ground out.

"Father believes you will see his side eventually. He has ever been ambitious for himself, as well as for you."

Valentine swallowed. "He will be sorely disappointed."

He caught Melanie's hand again. Her skin was ice cold, and after a moment she withdrew from his touch. "As much as I'd like to stay, I should be going before Father remembers I did not follow him. It's a miracle I've had this long to myself. He has been uncomfortably watchful of late."

"I'm sorry."

"He is the way he is." Melanie approached the door and opened it a crack. She turned back suddenly. "But before I go, I should like to say congratulations again. You've made a wise decision in marrying Julia. I hope you will both be very happy."

"Thank you." He moved to her side and kissed her brow. "No, I told you *so's*? I thought you'd ring a peal over my head for taking so long."

"Not today, and I'm sure my insistence had no impact on your decision. You have ever been a man to make up your own mind, in your own time." She stepped out into the hall but stopped to curtsy. "Mr. George."

"Miss Merton." George bowed formally. "Felicitations for your birthday last month."

His sister blinked and then she nodded. "Thank you, and the same to you of course."

Valentine frowned a moment, then he groaned. "Damnation, I forgot you share a birthday. Happy Birthday."

A fleeting smile crossed her face. "It wasn't important."

George gestured to the front door. "Your maid and a footman have arrived to return you to the hotel."

Valentine raked his hand through his hair as Melanie hurried away and disappeared. After a few minutes of staring, he sighed. "I should have gone with her. Made it up to her somehow."

George looked at him curiously. "How could you forget that your sister was of age?"

"I don't know, but I did. Christ, she'll never forget or forgive me for that."

"Perhaps your parents spoilt her or something." George shook his head.

"They likely wouldn't have done anything to mark the occasion." Valentine closed the door and sighed. "I should never have sent her back. It's no wonder she's having nightmares again."

When George said nothing to that, he glanced at his friend. George was frowning. "Go ahead. Say what is on your mind. I'm sure you, like everyone else, have enjoyed the peace while she's been gone."

"I remember you saying you believed sending her home was the only course of action. We all believed she'd make more trouble for Julia. Discovering that might not have been the case now is disconcerting."

Valentine glanced sharply at George. "You overheard us?"

"Not intentionally. The maid had come and…" George scratched his head. "I had no idea she wanted you to marry Julia. Everyone expected her to be furious about the match, if one was to be made."

"With me. She was angry with *me* about the race and the eventual damage that would fall on Julia. We quarreled quite heatedly over the matter. She insisted I had no choice but to marry the day I sent her away." Valentine shook his head. "When I refused, she begged me to at least consider it."

George squinted toward the door. "I thought she disliked Julia."

"Melanie does disapprove of Julia running about like a boy, and she has remarked endlessly about her habit of climbing through windows. It's unladylike, but that is as far as her censure goes. It probably sounds a great deal worse from her own lips though."

George shook his head. "That's not what I've heard."

"What have you heard, and from whom?"

George was silent a long moment then nodded. "I've been led to believe that Melanie finds the friendship between you and the Radleys an embarrassment."

"She doesn't. Has my father suggested that was the case?"

"Actually, no." George shook his head. "What Melanie said about your cousin Teresa stirring up trouble might be correct, you know. Over the years, most of the criticism about Melanie—and it's not even so easily termed, now I think about it—has come from your cousin. Melanie says this, Melanie says that. Melanie would not approve, etcetera. She is always quoting her. That is not to say your sister has always acted kindly, but added to the other, it has made her appear a shrew. Perhaps it is your *cousin* who does not approve of Julia. I shall have to look in to that."

"Don't cause trouble for her?"

"For Melanie?" George shrugged. "I don't think her reputation can suffer any more than it already has. However, if Teresa is misrepresenting your sister's opinions, I'd have thought you'd like to know for your own peace of mind."

"I do. I just don't want to cause another scandal."

George smiled. "I'll be discreet, I promise you."

Chapter Nine

Julia waited as Linus locked up the townhouse behind him. "Thank you for coming with me."

He snorted and fell into step beside her. "As if I could allow my sister to go to the market alone when there is so much at stake. You don't know how lucky you are."

She had an inkling of what her marriage meant to him. Now that she'd secured what he termed a proper match, Linus was even more determined that she behave appropriately. The fact that Valentine stole kisses and met with her after dark to talk had escaped his notice entirely. She held in a smile. If not for those stolen moments, she would never have consented to the match, ruined or not.

However, she would not argue with Linus today and held her tongue on the subject of her imminent marriage. If she thought of that coming day for too long, her stomach began to twist into knots. She would be Mrs. Merton soon. She glanced at her list quickly as panic assailed her again. "Mrs. Baker wants a pair of plovers today and whitebait delivered tomorrow."

"How long before the cut on her leg is healed enough to return to full duties?"

"Her foot," Julia corrected yet again. "A few more days, just to be safe. The last time she walked as far as the market it began to bleed. I do not like that, so she must rest."

"Do not speak of the matter to anyone."

Linus hated that while Mrs. Baker rested, the household errands fell to her to manage. She could have sent the scullery maid Julia had insisted Linus hire as additional help, but Mrs. Baker was so particular about whom she purchased from and the girl always went to the wrong stalls.

"Oh look, I see Miss Long is coming toward us," Linus said as they neared the first market stall. "And your betrothed is at her side. Hide that list this instant and pretend we are merely passing through."

"They are out early today," she murmured as she tucked the scrap of paper inside her glove while keeping an eye on their progress. Miss Long smiled suddenly. She faced Valentine, her face lighting up with joy as she spoke to him. Then she caught his arm and dragged him laughing into a nearby haberdashery shop. The door closed slowly but Valentine never had a chance to see them because his attention was riveted to his cousin.

Julia's feet turned to lead and she turned away to stare into an apple cart. She ignored the growing ache in her chest as she inspected the apples until her worry abated. The cart's owner moved closer. "How much for a pair?"

The old woman smiled. "A shilling for you, lovey."

She paid over the coin gladly and dropped the firm fruit into her basket. "Thank you."

She found Linus unsmiling, hands on his hips. "I swear they saw us. At least Miss Long recognized me."

"I'm convinced she did too." Too certain. When Julia added up the subtle snubs over the past weeks and months, she could not help the inevitable conclusion she came to. Teresa was no longer her friend. She had somehow lost her regard and likely it was because of Valentine.

"We should catch up to them."

"No," Julia protested as she retrieved her list. "I have all this to organize before luncheon for Mrs. Baker or she might come looking for me."

Linus grimaced and then relented. "Very well. But let's be quick about it."

"Miss Radley!" Melanie Merton called and Julia spun around, quite unused to the sound of Melanie raising her voice, especially on a public street. The woman rushed over, her maid trailing behind. "I was afraid you would not see me."

"Good morning."

They exchanged pleasantries and comments about the weather then Melanie grasped her arm. "I was hoping to call on you today but you were not at home?"

Julia glanced at the arm twined about hers so familiarly and then at her brother. Would her next words spoil this friendly meeting? "I'm running errands for cook."

"On account of her sore leg." Melanie winced. "Hmm, Valentine's housekeeper mentioned there had been an accident in your kitchen. I'm glad to see you've managed to make her rest."

"It has been quite a battle," Julia informed her.

"I imagine so." Melanie laughed softly and looked toward the paper. "What does she require this morning?"

Reluctantly Julia unfolded the sheet, aware that Melanie was scrutinizing her cook's shopping list with a critical eye.

"Do you mind if I join you?" Melanie asked suddenly.

"Yes, of course you may join us," Linus agreed before Julia could finish gaping like an idiot. What on earth would Melanie want to visit the market for? Shouldn't she be shopping with Valentine and Teresa Long?

"Thank you, sir." Melanie spoke to her maid quietly and handed over a coin. The maid smiled warmly and slipped it into her glove then peeked around the stalls nearby to see what she might buy.

"I find myself at a bit of a loose end this morning, so I am very glad you could accommodate my request," Melanie murmured quietly.

They moved deeper into the crowded marketplace. Heads bobbed deferentially to them, much more than normal, and it seemed to Julia that Melanie must be a well-known face here.

"Where is your father today?"

"He's gone to visit an old friend in Hove. Do you know the Markhams?"

"No. Not at all." She stored the name in her memory for

future reference. "Are they important people?"

"To my parents, yes." Melanie examined a loaf of bread, testing the weight with one hand. She paid over coin and the shopkeeper handed her purchase to a small lad of about ten. "Mr. Markham attended school with my father. They meet every time he comes to Brighton."

"What is he like?"

"He is exactly like my father, unfortunately," Melanie sighed. "I am glad to have been made to stay behind, I assure you."

Melanie stopped at several stalls Julia did not normally frequent and as she listened, she heard Melanie mention her brother's name frequently and his respect for their wares many times. So often that she came to realize Melanie was using her presence for a purpose.

At the end of her errand, Melanie took her arm and sighed. "That was perfect."

"You were promoting your brother."

"I must take every opportunity while I have the chance. When my father returns from Hove, I may not have the opportunity again. Knowing him and his whims so well, he could very well uproot us tomorrow."

"I wouldn't like that."

"Neither would I," Linus cut in, breaking his silence. "It has been good to see you again. Julia has missed you."

Julia tried not to reveal how great a lie that was.

To her surprise, Melanie smiled a little sadly, as if she already knew that wasn't the case. "I am sorry if my overfamiliarity has made you uncomfortable but it is the fastest way to disprove that I have any reservations about your marriage to my brother. Often it is not what is said but what is done that sticks in the mind."

"I see." She swallowed nervously. "Then perhaps you could help me."

"With what?

"To be more like you." Julia lowered her voice. "Graceful, calm. You have the respect of everyone you meet, where I do not."

They were outside Julia's home when Melanie turned to Linus. "Mr. Radley, might I steal your sister away for an intimate tea at my brother's home?"

He smiled broadly. "Yes, of course you may. Do please take her with my blessing."

Startled by his easy acceptance, Julia followed Melanie into her future home. At the door, the butler took their hats and gloves and set them aside. "Is my brother at home, Forbes?"

"No, miss," he apologized. "I thought he was meeting you."

"Our paths did not cross, unfortunately. Would you mind serving tea for myself and Miss Radley in the parlor in thirty minutes?"

"I'd be very happy to, miss." Forbes beamed. "Mrs. Vant and I were just saying that it's a pleasure to see you back in Brighton but we'd be happier yet to look after you at home."

"And I've missed you both very much."

Melanie watched the butler go with a smile, then whispered. "The reason I'm so well accepted in town is because I'm not in the habit of revealing my unmentionables to everyone. I hope you are done with that nonsense."

"Yes, well." Julia blushed. "That is in the past. I proved my point."

"But not the whole of what you'd intended."

Julia nodded numbly, expecting further criticism.

"It is difficult to be accepted by all. I certainly do not claim to be an expert but we can do better."

Julia turned into the parlor and glanced around. "Even so, the people who matter to Valentine's career like and accept you. I couldn't help but notice how you adroitly dropped his name into every conversation today."

"I make a point of currying their favor for his sake whenever I can. I've known of his intentions with regards to his career for a very long time. It wasn't easy at first but I learned to frequent the craftsmen's shops, buy their wares, and praise them at dinners. I discuss topics relevant to the running of the household with wives and sprinkle in a recommendation or two."

Julia nodded. "Teach me how to do that?"

"I don't think that is something I can accomplish over tea. You have to practice."

"Then what do you recommend? I've unintentionally made

things very difficult for your brother and I want to make it up to him."

Melanie nodded. "Well, my first piece of advice is: walking is not a race."

"I don't walk too fast," Julia protested, hands punching her hips.

"You do." Melanie gently nudged her hands from their position. "And don't stand like that either. It is not at all ladylike."

Julia uncurled her fingers and let her hands drop. "What else?"

"Walking first." Melanie turned her toward the other end of the hall and nudged her to pace the length. She did but when she turned around, Melanie was shaking her head. "Slower this time."

"I have long legs," Julia grumbled, stumbling through the mincing steps Melanie demanded she limit herself to.

"Shorter than mine, and I can manage perfectly well without sprinting everywhere I go."

She glanced up at Valentine's sister and although she wished to refute the claim, she had no choice but to agree with her. Melanie was half a head taller than herself and she always appeared so graceful. So perfectly poised. If Melanie could walk this way, so would she. Eventually. "I see your point."

"I'm not asking you to do what I would not do myself. You don't have to listen to me at all if you'd rather not." Melanie worried her lower lip, frowning. "But you did ask for my suggestions and this is where I feel you should begin."

"No, I will manage." Julia tried again and managed a fair imitation of Melanie's stride, enough so the woman actually smiled when she turned around.

"Much better. Sometimes it is preferable to walk at a slower pace. For instance, to make a journey longer for extended conversation; to show yourself off to your advantage; to hold a conversation where you have a chance to bring Valentine's interests into the discussion."

She paced up and down the hall again, earning generous smiles from Melanie. And it was easier to walk slowly while speaking. After recent events, Julia had preferred to go unnoticed about Brighton. The number of smirks that had been aimed her way was infuriating and she'd adopted the habit of hurrying from engagement to home without stopping.

When tea was brought into the parlor, she was satisfied with her progress and flopped down on a well-padded chair with a groan.

Melanie raised a brow. "That won't do. Only ever do that around your closest friends."

She laughed. "I thought I had."

Melanie let her remark pass without comment. She sipped her tea and Julia studied her poise. Perhaps she *had* been a little too casual at times.

"I thought I would only have to please Valentine," she murmured.

"Who's to say I am not already pleased?" Valentine cut in. "Hello, you two. What a happy surprise to find you here, and together."

Julia flushed pink at being caught speaking of her intended and glanced down at her teacup as Valentine kissed his sister's cheek. "Were we not to meet this morning?"

"You didn't come," Melanie said softly.

"You had already gone out," he countered.

"You were with Teresa in the market," Julia interrupted. "I saw you with her and I thought she saw me."

"She never said so." The siblings exchanged a long glance. "I am sorry to both of you. No snub was intended, I swear."

Melanie sighed. "Miss Radley and I actually found each other in the market this morning and passed a happy hour visiting stallholders there."

Valentine beamed. "I trust all went well."

"Very well. Each and every one we met spoke well of your imminent marriage."

Valentine eased into the chair beside Julia and caught her fingers. "My secret weapon, my dear sister's faith in me. I don't deserve her."

Melanie stifled a short laugh and then sobered. "Might I venture upstairs?"

"You do not need to ever ask that," he promised.

Julia frowned as Melanie swept from the room. "She has changed."

"No, she hasn't really but she is trying. And my behavior has disappointed her too."

Julia caught his hand and squeezed. "Sisters are very forgiving."

When Valentine leaned in to kiss her, Julia allowed the impropriety. It had been the most revealing morning of her life. She was not a good student but Melanie had more patience than she'd given her credit for.

When she drew back, Valentine's eyes were dark with mischief. "What have you and my sister been chatting about?"

"I asked for her help. I do need to impress the company; to do what she does for you seems daunting."

His eyes glowed and he kissed her again. "Don't change too much."

"Easy for you to say. You're not expected to glide into a room, float onto chairs or carry on inane conversations about the weather." She despised young women who acted as if a serious thought had never occurred to them. "Where did you go after the market?"

"Oh, here and there. I ran into an old friend from school after I took Teresa to the hotel and got to chatting about our fathers."

"I see."

Valentine kissed her softly. His fingers curved around her face and he looked deeply into her eyes.

Julia trembled at what she saw there. "Your sister is here," she whispered.

"My sister was kind enough to retire upstairs. Her door closed." Valentine eased her into the seat back gently and nibbled on her neck in that way he had to make her senses leap. "She won't disturb us."

His teeth grazed her neck and although the sensation was lovely, she pushed him away. "Valentine. We shouldn't."

"I know." He met her gaze. "But you do want to be wicked with me."

"Yes, but I don't want trouble with your sister today. Not after she's been so kind."

He brushed a hand down her arm and settled over her hip. "No breeches today."

"Not today." She adopted a haughty posture. "I was

attempting to be a lady."

Valentine's slow grin set her heart racing. He caught her gown and slowly revealed one leg up to her garter. His touch was gentle on the ribbon and her heart began to clatter against her ribs violently. "A very tempting morsel indeed."

He kissed her again, firmly, his hands eager on her thigh and elsewhere. When his touch wandered toward her breast, she gripped his wrist to stop him. Her resistance seemed to inflame Valentine, for he kissed her with such abandon that she was having trouble remembering why she should not be allowing it.

The front door closed loudly and Julia froze. They both turned at the sound and when Julia glanced past Valentine's head, she saw Teresa Long standing at the doorway.

Julia tugged her skirts back over her knees, blushing furiously.

Teresa paled and looked away. "I thought you said you would be out, Val."

"Change of plans." He stood, apparently unaffected by the interruption. "What brings you back?"

"I was worried about where Melanie had gone. She's not returned to the hotel."

"She's upstairs, in her room I believe. Let me go and fetch her." He hurried out, taking the stairs two at a time by the sound of it.

Teresa's glance in her direction was cold. "Well, if you would excuse me."

"Teresa, wait." Julia scrambled to her feet, straightening her gown as she went. Valentine's lovemaking had managed to twist it around her body.

Teresa looked her up and down scornfully. "I don't believe I have anything to say to you. How cunning you are to appeal to his base instincts as a means to better yourself."

"We are to be married," Julia insisted.

"Are you foolish enough to think so?" Teresa sniffed. "You don't know Valentine like I do, or the family. You don't understand what drives him. What is best for him."

She turned on her heel and disappeared upstairs, leaving Julia alone. Julia did know what Valentine wanted for his life and from her.

She lowered herself to her chair, picked up her teacup and eagerly awaited Melanie's return. The first time she'd ever done so.

Chapter Ten

Mr. Faraday grimaced. "I've had a very interesting day, sir."

"Oh?" Valentine glanced around the immaculate shop front of Faraday Clockworks, a premises he'd hoped to continue his own business in after Mr. Faraday retired. "What made it so?"

Faraday set aside a coil of fine wire. "I met with your father today. Quite by accident, he said it was."

Valentine's stomach lurched. "Is that so?"

"It is indeed." Faraday squinted at him, a sign his vision was growing worse. "You failed to mention your family disapproved of your chosen profession."

He sighed. What was the point of evasion when there was little chance of a good outcome? "My father prefers that I follow in his footsteps and return to Oxford to teach."

"But you don't want that? How strange." Faraday rubbed at the nicks and scars on his fingers. Signs he'd toiled at labor all his life. "It would be an easier employment than mine. A life of comfort and instant respect."

"I never have wanted an Oxford profession but he refuses to listen." Valentine replied bitterly. "The pompous idleness of academia disgusts me. I'd rather be useful than imagining I'm bettering young minds by bellowing at them every day for the rest of my life."

Faraday's mouth curved upward at his ferocity. "Have you been holding that in for a while?"

"Not exactly." He grinned sheepishly. "My sister has always known my feelings on the subject. It was she who suggested clock-making as an alternative career when you professed me so good at it."

Faraday nodded. "And your friends? What do they know of your grand plans?"

"My friends were the first admirers of my creations and they know I prefer a life in Brighton."

Mr. Faraday squinted at him. "And what does Miss Julia Radley have to say, now that her future position in society will be reduced by your going into trade? Surely she must want the better life afforded by a position in Oxford."

"She was not in the least bothered by the drop in status. In fact, she asked a great many questions about how the business would be run yesterday. I had not expected her intimate involvement but she seemed open to the idea. I explained about the long hours each day and the uncertainty of my income. I believe she understands the challenges ahead."

Faraday nodded slowly. "There's a lot of talk about Miss Radley."

"I'm sure there has been, but I have spoken to the vicar and the banns will be read on Sunday. We will be married as soon as we possibly can."

Faraday shuffled a crate back under the bench. "That's not the talk to which I was referring. Word has it she's come into some money and most likely will cry off before the banns are read."

Valentine frowned. "Who on earth told you that?"

"Your own father. He paints a lurid picture of her character. 'Grasping adventuress' was the kindest description. He gave me no reason to doubt his claim that she took his money to make a better life for herself, rather than marry you."

"The Radleys have received no additional funds." He racked his brain for a reason to account for his father's claim—and then swore. "A private word indeed. Now I know why my father insisted on a private meeting with her when he arrived."

"I take it the money might be fact." Faraday picked up a bit of brass and rubbed a rag across the surface briskly until it shone. "Additional funds would certainly help you in the transition. It takes time to build a reputation."

"So it does, and a cunning word in the right ears to ruin one."

"All too true, sadly." Faraday winced. "In light of these new facts, I'm afraid the company has imposed a new condition on your application. We want to meet her."

"Meet Julia? Whatever for?"

"Those who throw stones always have something to hide, but so often there is truth behind the slander." Faraday tossed the cloth and set the brass aside. "Bring your sister and perhaps that George fellow. Your neighbor, isn't he? They've known Miss Radley the longest and can offer opposing views of her character. Her brother's presence is not required. Tonight, here at six o'clock after closing hour."

"Yes, of course. I'll speak with her brother and see if Radley will accept my sister as chaperone for the meeting."

Faraday smiled tightly. "My wife, and the other wives, will be present if that's any comfort to him."

"It will be lovely to see them again. We will be here promptly, I assure you." But Valentine's mind raced. Why would the members' wives be coming with their husbands? Usually they were not involved in business discussions.

After saying goodbye and stumbling down the stairs in his haste, he ran directly into Teresa. He apologized profusely for not seeing her at first and glanced around for his father or Melanie. There was no one else about though. "What are you doing here alone, cousin?"

"I had to speak with you urgently." She glanced back at the shop he'd left and worried at her lip. "Father does not know I've slipped away."

Concerned by her expression, he caught her elbow and steered her back toward the hotel. "Is everything all right?"

She leaned into his support as they moved along. "Everything will be fine when this dreadful situation is over."

He smiled. "By next month, we will be on a steady course again."

"First the race, and now she has set you and your father at

odds. It causes a strain on all of us. You've made the right choice."

"What are you talking about?"

"You *are* going back to Oxford tomorrow with us."

Valentine dropped her arm in shock. "I'm not returning to Oxford."

"But Father said—"

"My father is wrong. And for your information, Julia has nothing to do with my disagreement with him. I have given the future considerable thought. I know what I want and it is a life here."

Teresa's eyes widened. "And with Julia, of all women?"

"I wouldn't have proposed a marriage between us if I didn't see the advantage."

"I hardly think going into trade an advantage." Teresa pressed her hand to her stomach and he noticed a pretty new reticule dangling from her wrist. "I wish you'd consulted with me before things had gone so far. Mother and Father will never welcome her."

He sighed again. "That was a possibility with anyone not of their choosing. Mother will accept her or she will never see the grandchildren she professes to want so terribly."

Valentine frowned at Teresa, puzzled that she couldn't be happy for him. And then he took a second look at her hat, another new purchase he'd not received a bill for. His mouth grew dry. Where had she found the funds for a new hat and reticule? And a new spencer. "I like Julia very much."

At that, Teresa scowled. "She's *made* you like her by flirting with you."

Valentine burst out laughing and saw they were already at the hotel where his father was staying. He composed himself quickly. "Believe me, Julia has never once flirted with me. Quite the reverse."

Teresa's nose wrinkled with distaste. "That's just desire you feel. You can satisfy that on any street corner. Even return to the Bear Tavern for it. But a wife must be of higher morals than that sort of woman."

Hearing the name of his former Oxford drinking haunt on his cousin's lips surprised him but her talk of women of supposedly low morals sent a chill through him too. He'd met his first sweetheart at a tavern, the very one she named. He'd never confessed to anyone the disappointment he'd suffered at discovering Eve Summers, a custodian's daughter, had quit Oxford overnight. It had been before Teresa had come to live with them. "What could you possibly know of such matters?"

Teresa swallowed. "Mother said you spent a lot of time drinking when you were younger. She was very clear in her disapproval. I'm glad you never found a similar situation here in Brighton."

The tavern in Oxford had rented rooms by the hour to lovers with nowhere else to go for bed play. He and Eve had made good use of one.

"I see." Had Mother been filling Teresa's head with his youthful indiscretions? He was furious if that were true. Not even Melanie knew of the most embarrassing infatuation of his youth. He met Teresa's gaze directly and saw embarrassment. She undoubtedly knew about Eve. "What I do in my personal life is *my* business, cousin. You would do well to remember who has kept a roof over your head all these summers."

She blinked. "There's no need for hostility."

"Isn't there?" He folded his arms over his chest. Melanie's warning about Teresa was suddenly all too easy to believe as the truth. Teresa's habit of calling his parents Mother and Father too was beginning to grate. He leaned forward a touch. "Tell me, how long have you been a spy in my home? And don't bother to deny you are writing to my mother and father about me. Your own words proclaim you've been sticking your nose where it does not belong already."

"I'm not. Your sister feels very strongly that—"

"Misquote my sister at your peril," he bit out. "Melanie has known for years what I intended to do with my life and for your information, it was Melanie who had me draw up a plan for my business. She also insisted I marry Julia the very afternoon of our race."

Teresa glanced around nervously. "She is against the match. Everyone knows how she feels about that girl."

"I doubt anyone knows her feelings on any matter. She's not written to anyone but me, and as far as I can tell, no one has written to her. Someone else has been conveying a false report of her opinions and I think it is you." He flexed his fingers over his arms, furious that he'd not realized what his cousin had been secretly doing to Melanie behind her back. He didn't need to wait for Walter George's findings to believe it. "Why would you be so cruel to her? She treated you as a sister."

"I told the truth!" Teresa tossed her head. "The truth no one sees. Melanie isn't the saint she appears to everyone else. She's greedy and manipulative and still everyone adores her."

"Not everyone adores her, and that is thanks to you. She certainly is not a saint but she's not against my marriage or my choices." Melanie had two large flaws, in his opinion. Often tactless and blunt, Melanie also went to pieces instead of helping the ill and infirm. "You cannot live in my home and speak ill of my sister to my friends. She has her faults, just as everyone does, but I will always see the best in her. Today, Melanie was offering Julia, at her request, advice on how to help me in my future endeavors. And what have you done? Sided with my parents, who want to drag me back to their stuffy, ordered world, and poured scorn on an honest and decent young woman."

"Valentine. Please! Just listen to me a moment. She's not as innocent as you imagine."

"Stop." He held out his hand to silence her. He did not want to hear from her the tale that Julia had taken his father's money or anything else. He knew Julia. "I've heard and learned enough. Choose carefully, cousin. It's time to decide where your loyalties lie."

"You're making a terrible mistake."

Valentine sighed. After all he'd done for Teresa, allowing her to live in his home because doctors claimed her health improved in the fresher sea air, treating her as a cherished sister and spoiling her as much as his finances allowed. How could she be so dismissive of his choices? "I don't believe that."

Teresa licked her lips and glanced around, clutching her new reticule tightly. He studied it and the blinders finally came off.

Teresa didn't care about him at all. She believed *her* life would be ruined by his choices. She'd chosen his parents' side to secure a comfortable life for herself.

He felt sick.

His revulsion must have shown on his face because Teresa paled, edged back a step and then fled into the hotel, returning to his father and his money.

Chapter Eleven

---◆---

Twilight had always been Julia's favorite time of day. She'd take stock of her achievements and make plans for tomorrow. Although now her tomorrow had to allow for her suitor. She glanced up at his face and saw a frown there yet again. "You're very quiet tonight."

Valentine squeezed her arm. "I am sorry. I have a lot on my mind right now."

"You're worried about tonight? I am too. What am I expected to say to them?" Julia asked again of Valentine, her stomach twisting in knots about the last minute invitation. She'd hoped their imminent marriage would appease the company but she'd never imagined she'd have to face them first.

Valentine shook his head. It wasn't the first time since his invitation to join them that he appeared confused. "I've no idea what they want with you."

"Breathe, and be yourself," Melanie advised again in a soft voice as they reached the end of a darkening street and the glow of the clockmaker's shop windows loomed ahead.

Julia halted and glanced around; even with night falling, she felt exposed. "I feel like everyone is looking at me."

"They are," Melanie agreed unhelpfully, "and you are doing splendidly, I assure you."

"Quite right," Mr. George agreed as well. "Don't fret until there is a need to."

Melanie squeezed Julia's hand and passed her by. She climbed the few steps to the door of the clockworks and waited at Walter's side as he knocked to announce their arrival.

Left alone with Valentine, she was gripped with panic. Tonight was so important to him. She couldn't dare make a mistake now.

Valentine smiled at her, a dazzling smile full of warmth and comfort and secret wickedness. He caught her hand, as he liked to do so often, and dragged her toward his sister.

Tonight, Melanie exuded the confidence Julia lacked and she scolded herself for not living up to her better example. She pasted on a smile and ascended the stairs just as the door opened to admit them.

Mr. George grinned as he held the door and allowed her to pass inside ahead of him. Since he'd trailed along largely in silence at Melanie's side the whole distance from home, she wasn't sure what he thought of his invitation but he didn't seem perturbed about his inclusion.

She stopped in the center of the shop and glanced around. Valentine had explained that he hoped to take over this shop when Mr. Faraday retired in the next year. It was exactly six o'clock and the sudden clamor of a dozen or more chiming clocks brought a wide grin to her face. She had always wondered what it would be like to come here when they all chimed together.

She smiled at Valentine. "That's really quite something to hear."

"I only have five at home," he whispered. "When we have a shop, you can expect to hear that sound more and more often." He turned her as Mrs. Faraday appeared from the rear of the dwelling and welcomed them. "Thank you for the invitation."

"We are very pleased our request for a meeting could be arranged at such short notice." There were two other men, and their wives she assumed, standing on either side of Mrs. Faraday. The men stared; the ladies glanced at her nervously as the introductions were made.

"Thank you for inviting me." She risked another smile,

wondering what was going on in their heads. Did they like her or not? Had she underdressed for the occasion? Had her hair become frizzy again in the evening breeze?

At her side, Melanie stirred and moved forward. "This is quite the gathering. Mrs. James, how well you look today. Mrs. Faraday. I trust your families are in good health."

"They are, Miss Merton. It's very good to see you back where you belong."

"I am happy to be here." She smiled. "Valentine has told me so much about his hopes for the shop and his affection for Julia too. I'm very pleased."

"It is obvious indeed." Mrs. Faraday gestured behind her. "Come. Everything is ready and waiting."

Valentine frowned then moved his arm around her back to guide her into the rear of the shop. A table in the rear workroom had been cleared and a selection of delicacies had been laid out on a pretty tablecloth. "Is it a party?"

"Yes." Mr. Faraday glanced around beaming. "It is my retirement."

Valentine's grip tightened but then he released her. "Why didn't you tell me earlier that it would be so soon?"

"I wanted to surprise you with the good news." Mr. Faraday passed over a glass of spirits and offered punch to herself and Melanie. "I received a most generous offer for the building. Too good to refuse, in fact."

"I see." Julia glanced quickly at her betrothed and saw his face had paled. He appeared devastated by this new development. "What does that mean for us, Valentine?"

He winced. "That I now have to negotiate with someone else for rent. It could cost more."

Julia caught his hand and squeezed. "I'm sure we'll manage the change."

"I'm sure you will too," Mr. Faraday said as he peered over his glasses and then winked at her. He passed Mr. George a glass and then raised his. "Mr. George, I want to thank you for ensuring this old man can be assured many long and comfortable final years."

They both twisted to look at the silent presence at their back.

George smiled at Faraday. "As I said to you. The building is sound and a good investment."

"Why would you do this," Valentine whispered in shock.

George shrugged. "I had the money to spare. Besides, the way your father was condemning the venture meant you'd never obtain a fair deal from a landlord, no matter how many conditions you met."

Valentine gulped. "You bought the building just so I would lease it from you?"

He nodded. "At the same rate until you're on your feet. Don't thank me yet. You have a lot of hours to put in before you're regarded as highly as Mr. Faraday and can match his income. Mr. Hawke manages my investments as you know and will set up the paperwork and handle everything between us. Shouldn't take too much time at all, I imagine."

"Oh, Walter!" Julia threw her arms around George impulsively and squeezed him for all she was worth. "You truly are the best man."

George extracted himself quickly, blushing. "You deserve this chance."

Valentine shook his hand but then scowled. "You might have dropped a hint."

"You're welcome." George glanced at those gathered. "So, I take it you finally agree to Mr. Merton's inclusion in your ranks?"

There was agreement all round and Valentine beamed. He gripped Julia's hand firmly. "Thank you. Thank you so very much from both of us."

"And I must thank Miss Radley. If my own health were better, I would have given chase that day instead of standing still like a blind fool. Brighton has become a dangerous place, but also dangerous for men with dishonorable intentions, with a woman like Miss Radley in our midst." Faraday took both of Julia's hands. "You have my undying gratitude for coming to my wife's rescue that day when I could not. Thank you."

Julia beamed. "I was honored to help in any way I could. You'd both looked so happy moments before."

He smiled too. "We're looking forward to your wedding."

"And the wedding breakfast? Have you made plans for that

yet?" Mrs. Faraday asked. She drew Julia aside so the men could talk about the business.

She gulped and then smiled guiltily. "Not yet. I haven't thought much about the wedding at all yet. Mr. Merton's proposal was very unexpected."

Mrs. Faraday shook her head. "To you, perhaps. The rest of us were waiting for this day to come, and high time too."

Julia glanced at Melanie helplessly, uncertain what to say to that.

Melanie smiled serenely and joined them. "The wedding breakfast is well in hand, I assure you, Mrs. Faraday."

Her words had the necessary impact. The ladies grew excited and then retreated to serve the men across the room.

Julia drew Melanie aside. "You shouldn't have lied to them. I've done nothing, and no one has even mentioned the wedding breakfast before today. I don't know what to do."

"It is done." Melanie nodded. "Cook promised me months ago that she and Mrs. Baker would divide up any cooking, compare notes on the menu, and ensure you a day you will long remember."

Julia gaped. "You organized my wedding breakfast before you left Brighton? How could you know I would accept your brother, or that he would even ask?"

"These things are best never left to chance." She smiled briefly. "We should rejoin the rest of the party."

Melanie moved toward the women and Julia followed, somewhat in shock. Hadn't she been told time and again that Melanie didn't approve of her? That she would stop at nothing to have Valentine wed to someone else? That seemed a vast contradiction to the reality she now faced.

She glanced at Mr. George, only to find the man staring at Melanie too. His brow wrinkled but then he glanced away to speak to Mr. Faraday, no doubt about the building he'd recently purchased. The pair laughed together and then moved toward a rear door.

Melanie followed at a distance and peered into a side room they'd just inspected. She spoke to Mr. George and it was clear her words were awkwardly received. She turned away soon after and rejoined the older women.

Valentine caught her hand. "I can't believe we've won through at last."

"I can. Didn't you say that together we could do anything?" She leaned into him a little, her happiness bubbling over. Now all she had to fear was the wedding night. Whatever that might entail.

That was something she didn't want to think about too hard right now.

After a little while, another set of clocks chimed and she was surprised by how the time had flown. "Eight o'clock," Valentine announced. "I promised your brother we wouldn't return too late."

She nodded then noticed Melanie was already bidding farewell to Mrs. Faraday. "Does Melanie have exceptional hearing?"

"No, but she does have a better sense of propriety than myself. She's been glancing at the clocks for a reason, not just to admire Mr. Faraday's work. Let's get you home so Linus doesn't grow cross with us."

Julia sighed and said her goodbyes then they filed out the door. She glanced back once, making a few plans for her own life with Valentine. She'd find a small corner of the workshop to claim. She didn't want to be in the way but she didn't want to be left behind at home every day.

Since it was dark out now, she drew near Valentine and they talked over the details of the shop's reopening under his leadership. Once, she glanced over her shoulder and noticed Melanie and Mr. George were speaking quietly together. She hadn't seen them appear so easy with each other in a long time, and she was pleased.

"I'd like to celebrate," Valentine whispered.

Her spirits lifted even further. "How? Where?"

"Only with you." He leaned close. "Come and see me after Linus falls asleep."

Julia's pulse jumped. Linus could fall asleep in an instant if the circumstances were right. "I could slip out to the workshop for a little while."

"Come to the townhouse instead. I'll be waiting at the back door for you."

What he suggested was not without risks, to her reputation and to his. "I don't know. What about your housekeeper?"

"Forbes has the night off and I will take care of Mrs. Vant." He grinned. "Do I really need to be the one to dare you to do something potentially scandalous with me this time?"

Julia grinned, remembering how she'd pleaded with him right before he'd accepted her dare to race her in the ocean. "Very well. I'll meet you at your back door, provided you make it worth my while."

"I'll have champagne waiting."

Julia almost squealed with excitement and then cast a guilty glance behind her. Linus rarely allowed her to drink. "I love champagne," she whispered.

"That's why I purchased a few bottles earlier this week." He smiled warmly. "I have to return Melanie to the hotel after I leave you. Give me an hour and then come to me."

She squeezed Valentine's arm, excited to have a partner in scandalous behavior at last. So far, he'd never let her down. "I can't wait."

Chapter Twelve

<hr>

Valentine dragged Julia into his home before she said one word and quietly shut and locked the rear door. Small noises traveled far on a still night and he didn't want any interruptions. Not when he had stolen a moment alone with his betrothed for their private celebration. He was giddy with excitement for the future and he wanted to celebrate with Julia. "Did you have any trouble getting away?"

"None. Linus was half asleep when I returned and snoring within fifteen minutes of retiring. It's incredible the change in him, now we are to marry. He's almost pleased with me." She touched his arm. "Is your sister happy everything has worked out with the company?"

"I think so. George joined us for the stroll to the hotel so we didn't have a chance to speak privately." He raked a hand through his hair. "And my father was waiting and blathered about family responsibilities and settling for second best. She slipped away before I could even say good night, but I could tell she has something on her mind."

"And Teresa?"

"I did not see her." He wasn't worried about Teresa one bit. Not after discovering how she'd worked against him. He slipped his arm around Julia's back and urged her toward the parlor, where he'd lit candles and the fire in preparation for her arrival.

The room was warm and intimate. Perfect for improving their relationship. He wanted Julia to consider him her friend and future. He didn't want their wedding night to be awkward. "Champagne is this way."

She clapped her hands and giggled at the sight of two champagne glasses set beside the open bottle on the small table. He poured and handed her a glass. "To disaster narrowly averted."

They clicked glasses and Julia sipped her beverage, her eyes aglow with mischief. She smiled warmly and settled on the settee. "I'm so happy that everything will work out with the company. How kind of Mr. George to help us."

"He was remarkably devious about it." Valentine sat beside her and reclined comfortably too. "George has some explaining to do tomorrow morning. Never a hint he knew what tonight was about."

"Oh, don't be too hard on him." She grinned and took another sip of her champagne. "Did you see how gentlemanly he was with Melanie tonight? He never used to like her very much."

"Because of how she reacted to Imogen's loss of sight, I imagine. She's never been very good around sickness, I'm afraid, especially when it involves our friends."

"She *wasn't* very kind about Imogen's lost sight. I truly thought she would hate the idea of our marriage."

He tipped his head as Julia started to fidget. "She doesn't. She's very happy about us."

She swallowed her champagne quickly and set the glass down.

Puzzled by her sudden nervousness, he set down his glass too. "Would you care for more? I must warn you, though, too much might make your head pound in the morning. That might be hard to explain."

"I had three glasses once." She laughed a little nervously. "Imogen conspired to help. My head hurt so terribly the next day that I vowed never to drink so much again."

He grinned. "When was that?"

"Hawke and Abigail's wedding." She sighed. "I miss Abigail."

He refilled her glass and handed it to her. "Perhaps they will visit soon."

"It's been a while. We should invite them for the wedding."

Valentine nodded. "I certainly hope they will come but it depends on Hawke's schedule."

Julia lifted her glass to her lips but didn't sip. "Marriage changes people."

She swallowed quickly, a sure sign of nervousness.

"It doesn't have to with us." He took her glass and set it back on the table. "I like you as you are, Julia. I don't want you to be anyone but yourself."

"Do you really mean that?"

He nodded and leaned forward to kiss her cheek. "Well, there are two things I'd have different: your name, and for your bed to be closer to mine—the very one in fact, so we could stop sneaking around and talk like this all the time."

He leaned back as she sucked in a sharp breath. Perhaps that was a little too blunt but with Julia, he thought he should be able to share his hopes for their life together. "Marriage means different things to different couples. My parents are not happy together. My father married my mother for her money. They are not in love. They do not share a bedchamber, hardly ever the same drawing room. I don't want that for us."

Julia touched his hand, her expression concerned. "My parents were happy."

"I remember them well. The way your father adored your mother was something to admire."

Julia glanced down at her empty fingers. "Neither one of my parents would have dared misbehave like this though. I'm not much like them."

"I'm not either." He traced the edge of her jaw to her full lower lip with the tip of his finger. "Not with you. When I'm with you, I'm filled with any number of inappropriate thoughts."

Her face flushed. "Such as?"

"Are you wearing trousers again? How long are your legs?" He grinned. "Can I steal another kiss? Or more?"

"More?"

He touched her cheek, brushing his thumb over the burning crest. Her breath was fast and her eyes glowed with something he dared hope was desire. "Everything. I want to share everything of myself with you."

"I'd like that too." She turned and sought his mouth. He held her to the kiss, deepening it when she fell against his chest, her arms twining around his neck. This was no stolen moment but the beginning of their life together. He held her close, loving her strength, her eagerness for new experiences. Her reaction told him everything he'd always known deep down.

He'd made the right choice to marry her because he loved everything about her.

He *loved* Julia's wildness. He didn't ever want to see her tamed.

He cupped her rear with both hands but Julia captured his wrists and pushed them aside. "Not so fast, sir."

He stared at her a moment then pushed back. She fought to hold her ground and in the struggle, he slipped beneath her on the settee. He took in his predicament and then grinned widely. She was half on top of him, which had not been his original intention, but aligned with his hopes for the future. "Not that I don't love tussling with you but now you have me, what are you going to do with me, my dear?"

She appeared startled, and her hands flexed around her wrists. "I don't know."

She shifted, moving her lithe body flush against his. The pose provoked him and, unable to resist, he lifted his hips and brushed against her sex with his growing arousal. "We could wrestle all night if you want."

"Wrestle?" Her lips parted, and when he did it again with clearer intent, she gasped.

"I don't need to be on top if you'd prefer the honor." He lifted his head to claim a quick kiss. "Do you remember the other day when I was teaching you to defend yourself? I had my arms around you so tightly. I wanted to kiss you then. Did resisting me excite you?"

She sat up quickly and nodded. "But that's wrong. If we're to be married then I shouldn't fight with you."

"If we are to be married, we can do anything we like with each other." He sat up and captured her lips. "Any way we like. Any time of day or night."

He got to his knees beside the settee. He caught one wrist and then the other in a light grip, but his intent was there for her to see. When he tried to move her hands, she denied him. "I love how strong you are," he whispered. "When you resist it excites me."

Julia swallowed.

"I'd never hurt you, I swear. It is just play." He relaxed his grip a little. "Glorious, exciting play. I would never want you to be afraid of me."

Julia twisted her hands and broke away. When she shoved hard against his chest, he fell backward onto the floor, almost cracking his skull. He gave thanks for the thick rug beneath him. Julia landed on top of him the next instant and the air rushed from his lungs. She laughed, pinned his hands above his head and kissed him.

Her grip was light, so he easily freed himself, clamped his arms around her body and rolled her over. They kissed while they wrestled, changing position, crashing into chairs in their struggles to best each other. Passion rose sharply for him with every grunt and small victory she claimed.

They were almost at the hearth, Julia's hair falling from the pins, her thighs clamped tightly around his legs, when he drew back. A light sheen of perspiration caused by her struggles had brought out a healthy glow to her skin. She laughed as he untangled their limbs a little but didn't move to straighten herself. "That was fun."

"Delightful." He kissed her lips quickly, and then buried his face at her neck. He licked her skin, one long taste from the base of her throat to the edge of her hair. She shrieked and bucked beneath him. He drew back and admired his future wife. One knee was raised provocatively and the glimpse of her bare thigh caught his attention. "No trousers? I'm halfway disappointed."

"Only Imogen has ever seen me wear them," she promised, fiddling with the ends of his cravat, which had come undone while they'd wrestled. She removed it slowly, her breath coming fast as his throat was bared. His shirt gaped, and her eyes widened as she stared at his chest.

Since most of her hair was coming down anyway, he removed the remaining pins and swept his fingers through the wild shoulder-length curls so they spilled in an arc around her head. "Well, we'll have to rectify that when we marry. Have you ever wondered what it would be like to dress as a man for a whole day?"

Her eyes widened impossibly. "You'd let me? I could never keep a shirt or waistcoat for myself at home. Cook always pinched them back so I've only ever had the one pair of trousers Linus outgrew years ago. I've always had to hide them or wear them."

"I'll act as valet, and then have the fun of undressing you afterward," he said as he slipped his hand down over her thigh and stroked her bare skin.

Julia laughed again then caught his head, pulled him down over her and wrapped her body around his. She teased him with a gentle kiss. "I could get used to being like this all the time. No one scolding me to behave like a lady. I can't believe how much fun you are."

"I'm not surprised, but I am lucky to have a woman who is not afraid of a little rough and tumble. I like that about you very much." He kissed her hard, any pretense of gentleness swept away by her eager response. The temptation of her lithe body was too much. He touched her collarbone with the tips of his fingers, and stroked to the edge of her gown. Her fingers tangled in his hair as he moved on to cup her breast. When he gently squeezed the soft orb, her back arched from the floor and a low moan left his throat. He rocked his hips against her core and was gratified to hear yet another moan tumble from her lips. Oh yes, they had a great deal in common.

He unbuttoned the fall of his trousers but she noticed his attention had changed direction and stilled his hand. He dropped his head to her shoulder. Too fast. Too soon. "Forgive me."

When she said nothing, he lifted his head to meet her gaze.

A bright blush had swept over her cheeks. "I've always been curious. May I?"

"By all means." He liked that she would be so honest in her desire, despite her innocence and blushes. He eased back and when she pushed her hand into his open trousers, he groaned this time.

"So warm," she whispered as her fingers wrapped around him. She squeezed him as firmly as his grip on her breast, and when he flexed his fingers she mimicked him. Curious to see how far she would copy him, he stroked his thumb over her hardened nipple.

Julia teased the head of his cock, and he groaned heavily. There was only so far this could go before the inevitable happened and she ended up his lover before marriage. He grinned. Where was the harm if they both wanted the same thing? "It's all your fault for exciting me to the brink of madness. You can add temptress to your list of accomplishments."

She punched his shoulder when she realized he was teasing rather than complaining and then slipped her hand back down to touch him. Her brow furrowed with concentration as she stroked over his length and she then teased the head again with her thumb. He was hard and aching, undoubtedly the evidence of his desire was on her fingertips. She squeezed harder and he thrust into her hand once, unable to stop himself.

He slipped his hand to her thigh and slowly lifted her gown high. A quick glance confirmed that she was as red between her legs as the hair on her head. Her thighs were pale and slender, trembling at his touch. He caressed her skin gently to soothe her, listening as her breath hitch when he inched higher toward the apex of her thighs. He brushed over her core lightly and earned a gasp. He rubbed her red curls between his fingers and then tugged slowly so her lower lips might part.

Julia arched from the floor again. "Did you invite me here to make love to me?"

"No. I had not planned to." He moved his hand back to her thigh. "I just wanted to be with you tonight."

She smiled softly and stoked him again. "I'm not nervous at all, Valentine. I like the way you make me feel about myself. About us. I don't want to wait until the wedding. Make me yours tonight."

He rose to his knees, shoved his trousers off his hips roughly, and leaned over her. "Your dare was the best thing that has ever happened to me."

Julia—brave, headstrong Julia—unbuttoned his waistcoat, slipped her hands under his shirt, and drew them both over his head.

His senses reeled at her eagerness.

She flattened her palms over his chest and a slow grin curved her lips. "You are very finely built, Mr. Merton."

"And you, Miss Radley, are wearing far too many clothes. I want them off you now." He reached for the buttons on her gown. Thankfully they were in the front and he quickly parted the material, revealing a fine silk chemise beneath. Through the thin material he could see the pink of her nipples. He moved off her and stripped her quickly until she lay bare on his rug, her skin kissed by the flickering candlelight.

He kept his eyes on her while he kicked off his remaining clothes.

Julia was breathtaking. Pert breasts, tiny waist, and long slender limbs. She was also blushing all over so her skin glowed pink.

Valentine smothered her with his body, gasping at the scorching contact of her flaming skin. He kissed her urgently, and she moved restlessly against him.

He eased back again and slipped his hand between her thighs. She hissed sharply when he parted her folds. When he delved between with the tip of his finger, discovering her excitement had made her deliciously wet, she curled her face into his chest.

"You've no reason to be shy with me," he whispered. "We are both excited. Both eager."

He slipped his finger inside her a short distance, thrusting just enough that she relaxed. He slid up to her clitoris and circled slowly.

"What are you doing to me?" she whispered as he continued to tease her.

"Making you mine. Forever," he leaned down to kiss her curls.

Although tasting her cream and bringing her to completion with his mouth was tempting he wanted to join with her more.

He parted her thighs urgently, laid his hips between and moved into position. He hovered on his forearms and met her gaze. The flush of color to Julia's face suited her.

Valentine pushed into her as gently as he could, unable to prevent her pain or hold back. She squeaked out a protest, but instead of pushing him away, she drew his head against hers, encouraging him to make love. He cradled the back of her head with one hand and with the other he squeezed her bottom. When he looked in her eyes, he saw his own excitement, his own desires reflected back at him.

He moved in her carefully, determined to make her feel him, feel his desire and make her experience the same. Julia curled around him suddenly, her arms and legs rising to embrace him completely. They rocked, almost wrestling again but with his cock buried deep inside her body the sensations were intense. He was fast losing this fight against her allure.

He fought against her clinging embrace so he could thrust into her wildly, reveling in her warmth and heavy moans. There was no one like her in the world and he counted his blessings that he'd captured such an adventurous spirit.

When she gasped suddenly, nails digging into his back, he paused to look into her eyes. However, they were scrunched up tight and she shook and strained against him the next moment. Only then did he understand just how excited she'd been. She'd climaxed without any guidance from him.

When her body grew limp, he pinned her wrists to the rug and lost himself in her. She smiled sleepily as he spilled his seed deep inside with a hoarse shout, overcome by the most mind-melting release of his life.

He rolled them as soon as his senses returned, placing himself beneath her, and fought for breath. Julia cuddled against his chest—and then suddenly started to laugh.

She snorted and then covered her face with both hands.

He'd never had that reaction to his lovemaking before. "What's so funny, pet?"

She met his gaze solemnly but she seemed on the verge of another chuckle. She stretched out one hand and brushed over the rug's weave. "I was just thinking how much I have always admired how perfect this rug is for this room."

"I see. And now we've been intimate upon it…"

"It holds an even greater place in my heart," she said, suppressing a smirk. "It is indeed a very stylish *and* comfortable rug."

Valentine brushed her falling hair back from her face as she continued to laugh loudly. "It's the perfect size for the space. I love it too. But not as much as I love you," he whispered softly beneath her chuckles.

Chapter Thirteen

———◆———

"Melanie, how good of you to visit." Julia hurried to her future sister-in-law and kissed her pale cheeks. "I'm so glad you have come to visit me again."

She led her into the parlor, where the two women sharing the settee across the room, Lady Watson and Teresa Long, exchanged a glance full of sarcasm and then murmured a cordial if brief greeting of, "Miss Merton."

"Lady Watson." Melanie settled onto a high-backed chair, but fidgeted with her reticule. She shot a glance at her cousin. "Miss Long. What a surprise to see you here. I understood from Father that you were expected to be elsewhere this morning."

"No." Teresa fiddled with the sleeve of the new gown they'd just been admiring. "I told him I would call on my friends. Father must have thought it unimportant to tell you the particulars."

Melanie shook her head. "He is *my* father and he likely forgot what you said the minute you spoke."

Teresa's face flickered with upset at the cruel taunt but she soon masked it. "No matter. I've had a lovely visit and now it's time for me to leave."

Miss Long stood and gripped Julia's hands firmly. "I'm sure he will come around eventually. He only wants what is best for his son."

Julia thought the man cared very little for what Valentine wanted. It seemed Valentine was a possession to Mr. Merton, and she didn't like that idea very much. She saw Teresa to the door where a maid waited, actually very glad to see her go. She felt uneasy around Teresa, and her earlier insistence that her word to Mr. Merton would carry more weight than Melanie's had been a startling suggestion she couldn't place much faith in.

Melanie was the one he should be listening too. Mr. Merton should also be listening to his son, and wanting him to be happy above all else.

She turned back toward the parlor frowning and hurried toward the only two people she knew who were entirely pleased for Valentine and sat down. "It's three of us again."

"Not for long," Imogen said suddenly and then stood. "Since my help is not needed for the wedding breakfast, I'll be on my way too. Miss Merton obviously has everything well in hand despite her distance."

Julia jumped to her feet again. "Please. There is no need to rush off just because the plans for the wedding day are further advanced than I'd first known. I'm actually very grateful that Melanie spoke to her cook about it. I'd not given the matter a single thought but Mrs. Baker promises she's balanced the chores between the two households so they can enjoy the day, too, without being run off their feet."

Imogen thought about that and resettled herself. "Still very high-handed."

"He's my brother," Melanie murmured. "Did you really think I'd risk leaving Valentine to organize what should be the most important day of Julia's life? His mind is split between the marriage and the opening of his shop as it is. Making sure the little details important to women are not forgotten is a task best left to the housekeepers anyway."

Imogen smiled tightly. "When my brother marries, I would not interfere."

Melanie glanced away. "You wouldn't need to with Walter. He is very different to my brother and took excellent care of you, and his home, when you could not see to do it."

That might have been the longest conversation the pair had

managed in a year, and Julia was pleased. However, a chilling silence ensued and she was keen to break the tension. "I saw Mrs. Faraday in the market this morning, Melanie. She seems overwhelmed by her husband's sudden retirement."

"She's worried about his eyesight for a long time. A workshop can be a dangerous place." Melanie cleared her throat. "Julia, we need to speak in private if you don't mind."

"What about?" Julia shook her head. "I don't have any secrets from Imogen."

Melanie glanced at Imogen a touch nervously, and then fiddled with the strings of her reticule. "It is about my father and the money he tossed at you."

Imogen spluttered. "What money?"

"Oh, that." Julia shrank, eyeing Melanie's hands nervously. She must have brought the money with her in her reticule. "I hadn't quite gotten around to sharing that insult with Imogen yet."

Melanie winced. "I cannot keep the money forever. I don't dare leave it in my room to be found. I would not be able to explain where it came from without sending my father into a fit of temper."

Julia sighed bitterly. "You couldn't think of a worthy charity?"

"It *is* yours."

Julia sank back into the settee. "You want me to tell Valentine about it, don't you?"

"Shouldn't you tell him? It will be impossible not to say where three hundred pounds has come from should he discover it."

"Three hundred?" Julia nearly swooned at the sum. "So that's what my honor was worth."

"Wait. What?" Imogen gasped. "What are you talking about? What money is this?"

"Oh." Julia jumped to her feet. "Mr. Merton tried to bribe me not to marry Valentine as soon as he heard about our arrangement to marry. Melanie heard the whole embarrassing conversation."

Imogen glared at Melanie. "How dare he?"

Julia paced behind Melanie. "That's what we thought, and of course I did not think clearly enough at the time to throw it back in his face as hard as I could."

Melanie turned. "No proper young lady should ever expect to receive a bribe from their future in-laws. It's not your fault you are in this situation. It is his. I do think Valentine needs to know, if my father hasn't already told him."

"Oh, and he would too. Just to make trouble for me." Julia stared out the front window, furious with herself for being slow-witted that day. "I wouldn't call it off now, of course, so I'll have to tell him every humiliating detail."

"Why 'of course'?" Imogen asked.

Julia's cheeks heated beyond her control to stop the blush. She met Imogen's surprised stare and then Melanie's confused one.

"I, um." Julia worried her lip. "I just wouldn't."

If a pin dropped, Julia was sure it could be heard all the way to China. Although a low grin spread over Imogen's face, Melanie's brow puckered with the beginnings of a frown and then her eyes widened so far in shock, Julia feared the woman would faint.

Julia smiled weakly but Melanie refused to meet her eyes again.

"Would you excuse me a moment?" she murmured before she rushed away, and, concerned by her reaction, Julia followed after her quickly to explain.

She found Melanie in the dining room, staring out the window and into the rear yard. "Melanie?"

The woman held up one hand and after a few long moments, slowly turned. She slumped against the window frame, her expression defeated. "He promised me he wouldn't bring you any further harm."

Julia had not realized her ruin would be so obvious to others. She wasn't exactly ashamed of herself but she knew that proper girls would never have enjoyed a romp on the floor with their intendeds so much. Melanie certainly would never do it if she ever found a man to marry. She glanced down at her hands. "I suppose you despise me for being weak."

"I cannot believe he would do this." Melanie's fists clenched at her sides. "I will never forgive him for treating you with such disrespect! I thought I knew him."

Alarmed by her high color, Julia moved closer and pitched her voice low. "He did not harm me. He did not even seduce me exactly. We were celebrating his success and it just happened. I suppose I should not have gone to see him alone, and at night, but I am not sorry I did."

Melanie's stare was incredulous. "You should have been married first."

Julia nodded. "He will marry me."

Melanie bit her lip, appearing to struggle with her emotions. Eventually she said, "He knows the danger. What if something should happen to him before the words are spoken? What happens to your future then if he's ruined you for anyone else? You've already run the gauntlet of mean-spiritedness."

"Shh, shh, shh." Julia hadn't thought of any of that at the time but rushed to comfort Melanie, who was working herself up into a terrible state. The woman was shaking with anger and it was all directed at her brother. It was surprisingly sweet of her to be concerned but entirely unnecessary. "Don't be cross. He did not ruin me without permission. It was lovely actually."

Melanie took a great gasping breath and held her hand up to her mouth. "Well, that is something. I could not have borne any more disappointments today."

Julia rubbed her arms. "Tell me why you are angry with Teresa?"

After a moment, Melanie straightened. "My cousin likes to pretend that she is my parents' daughter, even to me, and I am tired of how she speaks as if she knows them so well. They treat her like a pet, spoiling her with gifts and such. She has no more value to them than what she's willing to do for them in return."

"I thought I had imagined her slip of the tongue."

"No, but we'll be gone tomorrow and then you and Valentine can both get on with your lives, with the shop, without any more interference from the family."

"I am sorry to hear that. I had hoped we could all be friends but at least you and I understand each other better now."

"We do indeed. I do wish my brother had waited for the wedding or at least for banns to be read on Sunday. A sister does not like to imagine her brother's armors." She shuddered, swallowed, and hastily pulled on the strings of her reticule, revealing the pouch hidden inside. "I have the money with me. We can see Valentine together if you like, and I can explain to him that our father caught you by surprise and that you'd never intended to keep it, as Father likely will claim."

"I'd like that. Valentine thinks the world of you."

Imogen edged into the room, her expression one of disbelief.

Julia ignored her friend for a moment. "If you'd not been with me that day, I don't know what I'd have done. I would have worried I wasn't good enough to marry your brother. You saved me so much anxiety."

Imogen drew closer, her gaze fixed on Melanie. "Are you saying you actually approve of the match, Miss Merton? Because I've been led to believe you'd tried everything in your power to stop it."

"Stop it? I told him to marry her three months ago." Melanie appeared shocked. "I disapprove of the circumstances, of course I must, but Julia has the makings of a good wife. He cares for her. I'm certain she might, one day, learn to curb her more reckless tendencies."

Julia grinned, remembering Valentine's assurances last night that she need not change. "I will always try to be the best wife he could ever want."

"Make my brother happy." Melanie drew close, her face serious and determined. "Because his happiness is all that matters to me anymore."

"I will. I promise." She laughed suddenly, as a warm glow filled her at the thought of her intended. She embraced Melanie quickly. "You won't even have to dare me to look after him."

Chapter Fourteen

Valentine met with his father in a private dining room in the hotel. He chose this place for the distance between them and his future bride. Lovely, gloriously wild Julia. His heart skipped a beat at the memory of her lying over him on the parlor floor, and the lack of concern that had given her.

He stood as his father entered the small chamber. As usual his father was dressed in stern black and white with a red-striped waistcoat to offset the bleakness. Immaculate. A figure to intimidate. Not for the first time did Valentine wish he'd been born into another family. One that embraced after a prolonged separation. Any affection had been left to the servants to dole out sparingly during his childhood.

Tea had been delivered, and small cakes, none of which he needed. He held out his hand to his father reluctantly and they shook in a perfunctory manner.

When his father sat, a smug smile graced his face. "I take it you've come to your senses.

"Yes, I have," Valentine agreed. He was done listening to his father. "I have given everything you've said considerable thought and I can't believe how much time I've wasted."

His father grinned. "I thought to leave tomorrow. I can delay a day so you can return with us."

"I'm not leaving Brighton. I'm not returning to Oxford. I don't want the life you and mother offer there and I am so tired of telling you both. We will never have this discussion again, sir."

A muscle in his father's jaw twitched. "She's pretty but only passably."

Valentine clenched his fists. "Have a care, sir, how you speak of the woman I love."

"Love," his father snorted, dismissing his claim with a wave of his hand. "What do you know of love, boy?"

"A hell of a lot more than you do. Did you and Mother *ever* love each other?"

"Do not speak of my wife," his father hissed, his face mottling red.

"Then do not speak of Julia. She will be my wife, and I will brook no discussion on the subject."

"A wife with an unsavory character will do you no credit."

"For god's sake, whatever past she has is with me. Do not ever make the mistake of thinking I was an innocent party to our scandal."

"I'm not referring to the race, but your lack of good judgment. To take on a wife with the morals of a fortune hunter is foolish."

"She's no fortune hunter."

"Then why does she have three hundred pounds in her possession? Tell me that."

Valentine swallowed the lump in his throat. Her dowry was much less than that princely sum. "I'm sure she doesn't."

"Then you don't know her as well as you believe. The girl is like all the others; a bit of coin goes a long way to turning their hearts in a new direction."

"What others have there been, Father?"

His father shook his head. "You should be grateful for the care we've taken over your future. Your mother and I gave it much more consideration than you ever have."

He stood and towered over his father, leaning over the chair so he could not escape. "What other women have you thrown money at?"

His father fell silent.

"Eve?"

"An eager trollop."

Valentine straightened, and turned away in disgust when his father laughed.

He'd lost his heart to Eve, or thought he had at the time. "So you gave money to Julia, too. To make her go away."

"Nary a word of protest," his father crowed. "Took it and kept it."

If Julia had taken the money then there had to be a good reason for her decision not to speak of it. He'd never believe her a fortune hunter. Quite the opposite.

He smiled and faced his father again. "I have bad news for you. Your plan hasn't worked this time. She's still in Brighton with no plans to leave, and she is mine. I have no doubts about where *her* loyalties lie."

"She doesn't deserve to share our name. It is shameless the way she carries on in public. Shameless, I say, and I will not have her throwing fruit at people!"

Valentine narrowed his gaze on his father. "You knew the good Julia had done for the Faradays, too, and are still determined to think badly of her."

His father sniffed in distain. "The wildness of that girl knows no bounds. You cannot bring her to Oxford. You cannot marry her."

"But I will marry her. And since I've no interest in returning to Oxford, it shouldn't bother you what she does. Our life is here. My future is here with her."

His father sneered. "You would hardly choose her over your allowance?"

"In a heartbeat." He held his father's gaze. "I would marry a woman I adore rather than some insipid connection of yours."

"Harsh words when the truth is more telling. She's just like every woman you've ever fallen under the spell of."

"That's a lie."

His father tossed his head. "How little you really know of the world. If you doubt me, ask your sister. She was there when I handed the funds over. She knows everything."

Valentine considered that. Melanie had always been forthright. "What right do you have to interfere in my life?"

"Every right. It is time to cease this ridiculous rebellion and take up your future, sir!" His father's voice rose to a shout.

Valentine was just getting started. "I have my own responsibilities now. To make my own way, and to protect my future wife from scurrilous men like you."

"Now you listen to me—"

"No. We are done, sir. I will listen to no more of your blather. Leave my Julia alone, leave Brighton, and never come back here again. There is no one who wants you here."

"She will be your ruin," his father predicted.

"Undoubtedly, after your talk, she'll believe I am hers." Valentine scowled. "I'm glad I finally got to see how ruthless you can be with my own eyes and ears. Goodbye, Mr. Merton. Go back to your university and the fellows who slavishly curry your favor. Give my regards to Mother."

He collected his hat from the side table and strode out. Undoubtedly he'd be cut off without a shilling. That would make life somewhat less comfortable, but they would manage well enough if they lived modestly. His plan for the shop had been drawn up with the likelihood of his father's disapproval taken into account anyway.

He hurried to the Radley home and knocked on the door. When he was directed to Linus instead, he grew alarmed. "Where's Julia?"

"Merton, do you believe me a tolerant man?"

He listened carefully but detected no other presence in the house. "Yes, of course."

Radley pinched the bridge of his nose. "Then why do you persist in trying to pull the wool over my eyes?"

"I'm not sure I'm following you. Where is she?"

Linus stood and smoothed his waistcoat. "Invitations to tea at your home will raise eyebrows, even when they come from your esteemed sister."

"Julia is at my home with Melanie?" He sighed. For a brief and terrifying moment, his father's insinuations about her leaving had seemed possible. He should have known better, especially after last night's activities.

"As if you don't know that already." Linus scowled darkly. "I cannot be fooled twice."

Linus had been fooled at least four times so far but it wasn't wise to gloat. "I was with my father at the hotel, saying goodbye. I've only now just returned. I had no idea Melanie had invited her to call."

Radley peered at him. "You do seem a little wild."

"It was not a pleasant conversation with my father." He winced. "Now if you will excuse me, I really do need to speak to Julia to ensure she's all right. I fear my father may have been unpleasant to her when they last spoke."

Linus shrugged. "She said nothing to concern me afterward."

"Well, then perhaps I have misunderstood him." He relaxed a little. "I'd still like to talk to her today, if I may."

"By all means. Your sister is a suitable chaperone for a few moments."

"Then I will see you at St. Nicholas's tomorrow when the banns are read."

"And at long last too." Linus sighed and led him to the door.

Chapter Fifteen

"Well?" Melanie asked as she settled into a chair and poured from the second pot of tea.

Julia flicked the curtain closed. "I can't see him still. Oh, this waiting is torture."

"He will be back soon." Melanie breathed a heavy sigh before sitting forward and holding out a piece of paper. "In the meantime, I know you won't lack for advice but the first thing you really must do after the wedding is invite these women and their husbands to dinner."

The list was intimidating, all the more because she had to make a good impression for Valentine's sake. "I don't know if I can do this alone."

"Of course you can. You have my brother, don't forget," Melanie chided. "Just remember, these women, when they get to know you, have exactly the same hopes and dreams as you do."

"They dream of besting Valentine?"

Melanie burst out laughing but quickly recovered her poise. "Perhaps not that, but having a happy, harmonious home, respect of their peers. They long for acceptance just as you do. It is what every woman wants."

The front door opened and banged closed and they both glanced toward the sound.

Valentine grinned. "Found you at last. What are you pair doing here again?"

"I wanted a private word and arranged to meet here instead of the hotel. I hope you don't mind." Melanie held out her hands. "I came to congratulate my future sister again and offer a small suggestion to ease her way before I depart Brighton."

"I don't want you to leave."

"Father insists on an early start tomorrow. Teresa supports his decision to go, so we will." Her smile was a touch tense at the mention of Mr. Merton Senior and her cousin. "I don't believe I will be allowed time to see you both again in the morning."

Valentine's gaze snagged on hers and she could tell he was struggling against the idea of his sister leaving again, and likely for good this time. Melanie had surprised her with her cunning and unflinching support of her brother's ambitions. The least she could do was make things easier for the pair.

She nodded, keen to prove that no matter what he decided to do, it would be right.

Valentine crossed the room. "Stay with us instead of returning to Oxford."

Melanie shook her head. "It's not necessary to say such things. I will be in the way, and so long as you do marry Julia, I will be happy."

He knelt and caught Melanie's hand. "Brighton isn't the same without you."

"Valentine. You should only worry about your future. You and Julia have a lot to do in the coming months and years." From her reticule, Melanie produced the bribe her father had forced on Julia and held it out to him. "Here, this will help you start your shop. Father forced it on Julia before she realized his intent. I've had the money all along but I don't want it either. It would have been yours anyway. Consider it a wedding gift."

The large pouched contained more money than she'd ever seen in her life. A third viewing didn't make the insult Valentine's father had delivered any easier to bear.

Valentine took it slowly, and nodded. He glanced at Julia, his expression troubled. "Father mentioned this today."

"We thought he might." She sighed and flopped onto a chair.

"He took advantage of my shock. I should have tossed it at his head like I tossed those oranges at that thief."

"I'd have liked to have seen that." He grinned and then glanced at his sister. "My future wife might value your advice from time to time. Oxford is such a long way away when hosting a dinner you're nervous about."

"Can I think about it?"

"Indeed you can," Julia answered, and then she tugged her pocket watch from Valentine's waistcoat pocket and stared at the hands. "You have until I finish speaking to form your answer. I hope you remember I'm not a complete chatterbox."

She looked expectantly at Valentine's sister and waited. Melanie didn't seem to know what to say, and Julia smiled warmly. Melanie had been the confident one. A seemingly unflappable woman. But Julia suspected she'd only ever seen the surface.

"I understand now what Teresa has said of you to others, sister," Valentine murmured. "How she twisted your words and made everyone believe the worst of you behind our backs. Let her have our parents' undivided attention if she is so desperate for their approval. She will one day discover how little comfort those expensive trinkets they buy her can be when they are given without love and only growing expectations."

Julia leaned forward in time to see tears fill Melanie's eyes. "Please stay. I would like to get to know my new sister and I cannot do that by letter. I promise to pay attention to your instructions and to try not to embarrass you."

Tears slipped down Melanie's cheeks and she turned her face to wipe them away. After a moment she turned back, her control restored. "I'm more concerned at being an embarrassment to *you*. I don't do well around people our age, but it's home. However, I can promise to keep out of your way and only step in if you need my guidance."

Impulsively Julia threw her arms about Melanie and kissed her cheek soundly. "We will become the best of friends, I promise."

Melanie fought free of her embrace and stared at her. "Do you want to know what I really want? I've always suspected you and Valentine possessed similar natures. Prove it to me."

"We will." Valentine pushed to his feet. "I'll inform Father that you will remain a part of my household indefinitely and make arrangements with the hotel for your luggage to be delivered here tonight. Since you are of age now, he cannot prevent it either. You don't have to see them again today unless you really want to."

"Thank you. I'd rather not see them. I've listened to more than my fair share of complaints lately."

Valentine pointed at them both. "You two better start making plans for the wedding now before the shop gets in the way. And I'd better go speak to Father again. Wish me luck that we don't come to blows." He grimaced and met Julia's gaze. "Come and see me off."

"I'll give you a moment," Melanie offered graciously before turning toward the pianoforte that had remained silent while she'd been away. Her fingers trailed over the keys lightly.

Valentine smiled and caught her hand as soon as they were in the hall. "I was so worried about you. My father went beyond the pale."

"He did. Melanie believes he may have done it before, too." She leaned in to him for comfort. "It's a relief to talk about it. I never wanted to cause trouble between you and your father and I was taken by such surprise by what he insinuated. He doesn't like me."

"He doesn't like anyone much, least of all his children. He doesn't matter now anyway. He might threaten to cut me off but the next in line to inherit his estate is a distant relative he considers a blithering idiot. He won't rush to disown me I should think." He kissed her brow and her legs trembled. "The banns will be read tomorrow."

She snuggled against him, wishing they could be truly alone and not just for a moment. "And in a few weeks I'll be your wife."

He stroked down her back and her breath caught as his grip firmed on her hip. "I wish it could be tomorrow."

"Why is that?"

He teased her cheek with his lips. "Because I'm in love with you and can't bear to leave you even now."

Her pulse raced at his words. He'd said he loved her last night but she hadn't liked to think too much about his declaration in case he didn't mean it the way she'd hoped. "I never expected that."

"Neither did I, and I must say, I don't mind saying it first." He kissed her lips softly, just a tease to remind her of their attraction.

Three weeks was such a long time to wait to be in his arms again. "What is it like to be in love?"

"Wonderful." He sighed as he tortured her with a lighter almost-kiss. "I think of you all the time. Wonder what you're doing, what you think of things and people. Soon I will be able to ask you anytime I like. It's an ache. I'm eager to be near you, and not just because of what we shared last night. I want you to be happy above everything and I think you will be with me."

She stilled in his arms and then raised her head. "That's how I feel about you. I can't wait to see what you will do or say next."

A pleased grin spread over his face. "Well then, I guess that means we were meant to be and perhaps I don't even need to dare you to love me."

He looked so hopeful she laughed.

"No. I really do love you without an incentive." She threw her arms about his neck.

Valentine hugged her tightly and then set her on her feet. "I'd best be going. Linus is getting suspicious about you being in my home so often."

"Gracious, does he know about last night too?"

"No. Who else knows?" He groaned. "Surely you didn't tell Imogen about meeting with me again?"

"I didn't have to tell them. They just knew."

"Who is 'they'?"

"Imogen and your sister, unfortunately." She winced. "Melanie was upset at first. Very angry with you, but I believe I convinced her I was a willing participant."

Although he did not look pleased, he squeezed her bottom. "A *very* willing participant. I loved that you were fully engaged in our romp."

She blushed and pushed at his chest to put distance between them.

"Tease," he whispered before grinning wickedly. "Keep challenging me."

"Always, Mr. Merton." She winked at him. "You can count on it."

———◆———

If you enjoyed Miss Radley's Third Dare
don't miss the next
Miss Mayhem romance

Miss Merton's Last Hope

Never-to-wed Melanie Merton had a knack for repelling suitors, that is until neighbor Walter George got close enough to learn her shocking secret. Although Melanie assures him there's no hope, Walter can't convince himself to give up on the promise of love.

About Heather Boyd

————◆————

Determined to escape the Aussie sun on a scorching camping holiday, Heather picked up a pen and notebook from a corner store and started writing her very first novel—Chills. Years later, she is the author of over thirty romances and has no plans to stop. Addicted to all things tech (never again will Heather write a novel longhand) and fascinated by English society of the early 1800's, Heather spends her days getting her characters in and out of trouble and into bed together (if they make it that far). She lives on the edge of beautiful Lake Macquarie, Australia with her trio of mischievous rogues (husband and two sons) along with one rescued cat whose only interest is that she provides him with food on demand.

You can find details of her writing at
www.Heather-Boyd.com